MW00620880

THE THING ABOUT MUSTARD SEEDS

The Thing about Mustard Seeds

By Kelly Sullivan Yonce

© 2020 by Kelly Sullivan Yonce

All rights reserved. This book or any portion thereof may not be reproduced or used in any manner whatsoever without the express written permission of the publisher except for the use of brief quotations in a book review.

ISBN: 978-0-578-64927-6

"*Truly I tell you, if you have faith as small as a mustard seed, you can say to this mountain, 'move from here to there,' and it will move.*"

—Matthew 17:20

CHAPTER 1:

Lace Dresses and Hard Lessons

osling, 1995—I was covered in mud from toe to tail, running the wrong direction in a dress I should not have been wearing. A simple mud puddle would have been easy to explain to Lula, but this dirt came with transgressions.

Every stomp of my bare feet into the earth shot more mud toward my once-pristine dress. It was a few sizes too big, since Lula hadn't taken it in yet. I was too deep into my offenses to stop running, so my ten-year-old logic told me to keep going until I circled back round the earth to reach the south again.

Lula always said, "You run long enough in this town, you'll end up back where you started like a boomerang."

I was ready to test her theory.

My Easter dress was torn across one of the cap sleeves. I loved those lace-trimmed cap sleeves. They complemented the chiffon perfectly. I didn't care for the green color, but the mud was fixing that for me.

Lula told me she had wanted to alter the dress before I wore it because I was "rail thin," which is not to be confused with "real thin." She tried her best to fatten me up, but my metabolism didn't give way to her attempts no matter how much lard she used in her cooking.

That morning she had brushed the naughty right out of my hair. Despite the long line of straight-haired brunettes in my family, I was born with curly blond hair, which in that moment was sprinkled with the dust of my ancestors.

I wasn't much for listening usually, but Lula made it darn well clear that I better not mess around in her closet. She was going to tan my hide, bust my britches, cut my butt, or schedule me a come-to-Jesus meeting. Any way you wanted to phrase it, I was afraid of getting spanked. Lula rarely spanked me despite frequently flirting with the idea. No matter how bad I was, at the end of every evening she would kiss me on the head while she laid me to bed in my clean pajamas and tell me I was her favorite granddaughter. I was her only granddaughter.

Lula would occasionally have that gleam in her eye that reverberated an "if I only could beat you" feeling through-out the room. I was betting she had probably saved up years of repressed spankings for this one incident.

The dress was the least of my issues. If it were only about the dress, she'd probably shrug that one off after fussing for a hot minute. Then we'd eat something, sit on the porch, and the sun would settle quietly on Liberty Creek Road like it did every other evening. However, I didn't see myself getting past the matter of Papa's ashes.

The ashes—the ashes alone—called for her cashing in on years' worth of whooping that I'd nary received.

Lula's closet was something to write home about. If I had another home, I certainly would have used the good stationary with the flowers on it. She used it as a prayer space and spent each morning and afternoon sitting in there with her devotionals and tea.

It had a small window overlooking the creek that met our small backyard. She put a small antique wooden chair by the little window and placed her tea on the little windowsill while she wrote in her journal.

The only other thing in the closet was shelving that was hand-painted by my Papa when he was alive.

The closet failed to fulfill its actual purpose of holding clothing and shoes. All of Lula's clothes fit into a dresser in her actual bedroom. Lula had a beautiful home. I wasn't sure why she had to hole up in a closet to talk to Jesus, but that was neither here nor there.

My dress was on the top shelf. I wished it had been on a hanger, but she stuck it up as high as she could because she knew I'd go for it. Why would she put me in danger like that, knowing I wouldn't resist?

I figured I was small enough to make my way up the shelves without breaking anything important. I shakily stationed myself on that first step and realized I was in over my head. Just a few more up and I'd be able to reach it. I was close enough to touch the top shelf, and I felt the trim of the dress on my fingertips.

I could hear Lula's voice in my head saying, "Stand up straight. Hold your shoulders back."

She was right in this case. If I had better posture, I'd probably already have my hands on the thing. I stood up a little straighter and tugged on the hem of the dress. It was working, and it pulled closer to me, but I simultaneously knocked over the big blue urn that held Papa's ashes.

I quickly covered my head, fell to the floor, and tried to avoid being knocked out by the urn. The urn hit the hardwood fast and broke into many pieces, leaving Papa's murky dust and bone fragments all over Lula's prayer closet.

My mouth and eyes gaped open, basically competing against each other for how big they could get. I was wondering when Lula would run upstairs and find me in my predicament.

Time passed and she hadn't arrived, so I shimmied out of my clothes and put the dress on over my head. Don't get me wrong. I felt bad about spilling Papa, but if I was about to die, I might as well be wearing a nice dress—this way they wouldn't have to change my clothes before they buried me.

With the dress on, I started using my hands to gather up his ashes into as neat a pile as I could, moving larger pieces of the urn into their own neat pile. I didn't even hear Lula come up the stairs.

She walked into the closet, and she looked around to assess the situation. Silence. I was already afraid. When she started counting, I wondered if she was trying to calm herself down so she wouldn't kill me or giving me a head start. I decided it didn't make sense for me to wait around and find out the hard way.

I ran down the stairs, and the screen door slammed behind me as I ran down the steps of our porch into Lula's front yard.

By the time my bare feet hit the lawn, she hung her whole body out the upstairs window and yelled for me to come back in. I wanted to listen, but I couldn't quite stop my legs from moving. It was like they were attached to the other end of a windup toy. You can try to hold them still, but they have a mind of their own. At first, the fear and adrenaline made me run like a madwoman. I kept going because I simply couldn't stop.

I ran down her long driveway, passing the entrance to the creek to my right, and I kept near the side of the bridged highway leading into the small main road through Liberty.

My arms spread out wide with my palms touching the nature around me as I continued my great escape. I looked up at the sky that touched the Smoky Mountain South and wondered if it fell on the land like that everywhere.

In the central part of town, I was met with shops and curious faces. I ran past Mae Whitlow from church. She was sitting outside of Liberty Grille reading a newspaper and eating fruit. She had her pretty golden hair hanging down past her shoulders and was wearing a white blouse, black pants, and sunglasses. She always looked like she had come out of a movie.

Eventually, my run became heavy on my feet, and I slowed to a jog. I became fascinated with my sunken toes and stopped running. My hands hit my knees, and I tried to catch a breath. I turned back around with every intention of walking back home to Lula, knowing that she was more likely to lecture than spank me.

I was by the main road into town, where the red covered bridge spanned from one end of the creek to the other. I followed the rocky steps down to the water to wash my face. As I turned back to the road, I encountered a snake in my path, staring at me as ugly as sin.

I don't know much about snakes and didn't think to wonder whether it was poisonous or if I actually had anything to fear. I was still scared.

I knew I didn't have a plan, but I thought maybe I could go around him. It began creeping in my direction. I turned again to run back where I had come from and fell into the mud, twisting my ankle.

It slithered around as I sat on the ground, moving backward, wondering what the most logical next step should be. The snake moved in my direction just as someone picked me up from the ground and pulled me out of its way. I landed rear end in the wet earth again, just in a better location.

The boy walked away shaking his head. He wasn't much taller than me and appeared to be close to my age. My hands sank into the mud to lift my body, and I chased him.

"Who are you?" I shouted this less-than-proper thank-you to the back of his head.

"You're welcome," he replied.

"I didn't say thank you."

"Well, maybe you should." He continued walking without looking back in my direction.

"You just threw me on the ground."

"You some kind of idiot?" he asked, still trailing away. "You were on the ground."

He was sunburnt beneath his short sleeves, and his tall, waxy boots met the bottom of his dirty khaki shorts.

"I'm smarter than most. And I could have handled that situation just fine!"

He spun around, and I noticed his jawline. His bone structure was very defined but coupled with big blue eyes and high cheekbones. I could tell that he had one of those faces where he likely always looked annoyed even when he was happy.

Freckles mocked his irritated angry face, taking his edge down several notches and giving his face a soft character that his rude disposition was desperately trying to avoid.

He looked at me, starting down by my ankles, and with disgust moved his glance up to my face. I realized how odd I must look in a muddy, oversized princess dress.

"I assessed you just fine. You're an idiot."

"Are you always this mean?"

I didn't realize how country he was until he laughed. The good ole boy in him was shouting from the rooftops. As much as I wanted to size him up and put him into his box, a complexity peered from behind his eyes.

He turned to walk away.

"What's your name?" I shouted to his back. "I'm Rosling Landry, Lula Landry's granddaughter."

Nothing.

"Hey, I asked your name. Are you some kind of hapless hillbilly? I asked you your name!"

"Gentry Lee," he said quietly as he kept walking.

I decided to follow until we reached the other side of the covered bridge. I hadn't paid attention to where I was following him, which ended up being farther away from where I needed to be.

I still don't understand why he couldn't bother to look back, and I started to feel offended.

Lula was right about people most of the time. She'd probably know exactly what to say about Gentry. I could hear her in my head, and I envisioned her walking around the kitchen while she gave me a lecture about who I shouldn't run with. I knew I should head back to Lula. Being around Gentry made me realize that Lula was a different kind of smart—a perceptive and wily champion of truth.

We stood by the side of the covered bridge, and Gentry finally turned back to notice that I was still behind him. Just as he opened his mouth to fuss at me, a truck drove past us so quickly that we must have looked like grass swaying in its dusty wake.

It came to a screech at a nearby house connecting to the creek, and my new best friend quickly pushed me flat to my belly and shushed me. That was the second time he put me on the ground that day. He joined me this time with curiosity in his eyes while he intently watched the truck.

I tried to lift up my body from the ground, but he whisper-yelled that I needed to stay down. Seconds later a man hopped out of the truck. It was a shiny blue two-door truck with a dream catcher hanging from the rearview mirror. The man was a southern kind of dapper in his light-green collared shirt, and I got the sense that money had done him good. His buttoned sleeves folded up to his elbow, and a tattoo of a catfish peeked out from the sleeve like it was swimming down his forearm.

I looked over at Gentry as he intently watched the man. He didn't break his concentration despite my nagging.

"Can I leave now?" I was asking rhetorically, knowing good and well I wasn't going anywhere even if he gave me his nod of blessing.

The man from the truck approached the front door of the house and knocked loudly. No one answered for a minute.

He knocked again, banging his entire forearm on the door repeatedly.

A man came to the door, and he was of similar stature. The man who opened the door held his hands out, facing his palms toward the man from the truck. They argued for a minute.

"Just get back in the truck. Go home." The man from the front door pointed at the truck and tried to shut the door.

"I'm not going anywhere." The man from the truck was yelling now. "She's my wife!"

I thought maybe the argument was coming to an end, because the first man walked quickly back to the truck.

But I was wrong. He grabbed a gun from the front seat and reemerged before the man from the house was able to walk back in.

I closed my eyes tight and started to scream. Gentry immediately covered my mouth and begged me to be quiet.

"It's okay; don't move. He'll see us. Just calm down."

He grabbed my face and turned it toward him. "Don't look over there. Don't you look. We are going to sit here quiet and then leave as soon as its safe."

Tears met the corner of his eyes as he tried to distract me from the situation. I shoved him off and looked back toward the men at the exact wrong time.

The shots fired loudly through Liberty that day. I couldn't shut my eyes fast enough, and I still saw everything, including dying man's final expression.

Every part of me tightened in fear. The first man got back in the truck and pulled toward our direction to go back to wherever he had come from. His truck zipped past us faster than it had arrived.

The other man was left lying in the doorway. I wondered what his last thought was.

Gentry snapped me back into focus.

"You have to leave. You have to go home," he insisted. "Don't tell a soul what you saw out here today, you understand?"

"No, I don't understand. Why wouldn't I tell anyone?" I yelled it at him knowing he was the idiot, not me.

Gentry started sobbing and grabbing at his hair. "That was my daddy. The man who drove off. That was my daddy. You cannot tell a soul."

He stood up and didn't bother wiping any of the earth off of his clothes.

The next moment is what I regret most about that day. I turned on my heel without consoling Gentry and ran back home. I didn't know what his plan was. I didn't know where he lived or if his daddy knew he was out there. I simply ran. Every breath of air felt heavy in my chest. Humidity covered the ninety-two-degree evening like a bad rumor, spreading its angst corner to corner of our town.

As I reached Liberty Creek Road, I could see Lula waiting on the front porch steps for me. The event had shaken me to my core. It suddenly made me remember Lula's goodness.

This made me run faster until I was close enough to jump into her arms. As I hugged her, I could hear multiple sirens in the distance as they screamed their way through to the chaos.

My mind-set had changed from earlier that afternoon. I knew Lula wasn't going to spank me even though I deserved it. She was one of the good ones. She was consistent and loving despite me being a constant handful.

I had always felt at peace on Lula's porch, but as she held me, I vowed I would never take her for granted again.

I wanted so badly to forget what I had seen. I wanted Lula to hand me a peach as I sat there in clean clothes while she fussed about me biting my nails or forgetting to turn off the bathroom light.

I wished hard for a clean mind that only knew about true human nature from a distance. Instead, I learned that day that every living being is given a choice between good and evil, right and wrong, and some of them are undeniably predisposed to choosing wrong.

Holding Lula reminded me that in her presence I was actually free. I hugged her so tight that she likely assumed I felt guilty about Papa's ashes. Or maybe she thought I was nervous about the sirens. Either way, she knew that I wished I hadn't run off. To Lula, in her gracious ways, me being upset and sorry was punishment enough.

Lula always said that a lie was like a feral cat. If you nourish the lie, it'll just get fatter and continue to lie by your feet until you trip over it. She was very deliberate with her metaphors. I had never lied to Lula before, at least not this kind of lie.

"Lula..." I looked up at her, and she stared at me like she knew I was holding on to a grenade. "I need to tell you something."

CHAPTER 2 :

Redemption at the Bingo Hall

Gentry, 2020—The steps of Liberty Bingo Hall were somewhat of a hazard. Cracked brick lined with vines led to the front door, which was in even worse shape. I wasn't sure if the wood was rotting due to water or termite damage.

I sized up the building's windows as I walked around the property and decided that most of them were only serving as a deterrent, but if the right criminal had a strong enough sneeze, they'd stand a fair chance at breaking through.

It was unquestionable, or so it had to be because I already signed the paperwork—this building was where I would house the church. The original sanctuary had been around since the 1920s. The pastor had been around since the 1950s. He passed away, and then, shortly after that, the building burned down. This meant for a brokenhearted congregation.

When I graduated high school, I basically disappeared from the town. I received enough grants and loans to attend a school in Indianapolis, Indiana. It was a fresh start.

No one there knew who my dad was, it was a relatively large city, and I had a chance to be something new.

My first year I was in a dorm with three other guys. They were messy and were awake different hours than me. It made it easier to fall through the cracks because we didn't cross paths enough for them to know me.

My classes were big, and I could easily blend. Sociology required a community service project, so I volunteered at a food bank, thinking I'd be able to cook or clean without much interaction and fulfil my class commitment. After several weeks of exchanging hot meals for warm glances of gratitude, I realized I needed the same restoration that they did. I started volunteering anywhere that needed help and somehow ended up working with Pastor Thomas.

He invited me to help with his outreach event, which happened to be at a pizza restaurant next to a liquor store. Pastor Thomas bought several large pepperoni pizzas and had them double sliced. Each time someone approached the liquor store, he'd offer them a free slice and prayer. The number of people who said yes to prayer surprised me. He never judged them and never told them to stop what they were doing. He never told them that they were on the fast track to hell. He simply provided pizza and prayer. Every person had a story, a need. They laid them down; he invited them to reach out again and come to his church, and many of them did.

I still remember his words. "It is my job to plant the seed and help them see the love of Jesus. Christ takes over from there." Over time, I started attending services and then switched colleges and majors to become a ministerial student.

When I thought about Liberty, I knew that I had old wounds that needed to heal, and I took a job as the lead pastor in my hometown.

I had only been back in Liberty for a few weeks. To make things worse, I was the black sheep of this town who had managed to turn himself around after graduating high school and moving away for seventeen years. Most of the church probably took it as prank when I walked through the doors to announce myself as their new pastor.

None of them bought in to my newfound relationship with Jesus. Nor did they think I was qualified enough to explain the gospel to them.

I was supposed to be showing Lula around the building to get her official "blessing," but she seemed to be running late. Liberty was a small town, and everyone knew my story. Lula was quick to look past it. She was the key to success and my key to making amends with Rosling.

Lula Landry had been with the church for her entire life and had watched it grow and then fall. She made it clear to me that she was loyal to her church and faithful to *her* Jesus, and she was hoping to help the congregation find their trust in me as their new pastor.

Lula told me that she had never in her life been late for anything, and I'd best not be late for anything either. As far as she was concerned, I was her apprentice, and she was going to teach me how to deliver this congregation to the Lord. Even though she was hard on me, I could tell she was invested in giving me a fighting chance.

The previous owners of the bingo hall had left me six long tables with seventy-two wooden chairs, most of them in need of repair. I also was the new proud owner of a slow cooker with dried-up meatball residue, a coffee maker, a deluxe bingo cage and bingo paraphernalia, and someone's old mattress. The mattress was perfect because I'd also need to make one of these rooms my temporary home.

After several years of classes to become an ordained minister, I started wondering why the coursework didn't include construction. I was handy with plumbing and electrical, and the rest of it would have to come together. If nothing else, I would build a great team. A great church.

I began folding up the tables and moving the chairs into a large utility closet. That was where they'd need to stay while we worked on the property. I was overwhelmed by the space and started making a mental to-do list that created a pit in my stomach.

Lula Landry was supposed to be arriving with Del Chase. Del was a senior in high school and played every instrument in our worship band minus the keyboard. Lula had been the piano player at the church for over forty years, so my first gift to her was a new keyboard since the old church's piano didn't make it through the fire.

Having Lula on the keys and Del leading the band was just one quirky part of our worship set. The most influential members of the congregation didn't like that the service was becoming more modern. Each set started with one hymn, per Lula's recommendation, and was followed by modern praise and worship.

Every now and again, Del would strum classic rock that went over most everyone's heads. Even though he was still in high school, Del was our acting worship leader.

The first set I watched Lula and Del play was in the living room of Mae Whitlow. When we lost the old sanctuary, Mae felt called to provide us a new temporary meeting space.

Other than being a self-proclaimed reformed gossip and harboring a hatred of me, Mae was mostly cordial. I couldn't blame her for hating me. Among larger transgressions, I stole her lawn equipment when I was fourteen. I can still see her standing in her pink, fluffy robe yelling at me in the back of the police cruiser. My only retort was that I needed the equipment for landscaping. Mae's aversion to me went deeper than petty theft, but neither of us wanted to talk about that much. It was the elephant in the room. Quite the elephant.

Lula's tardiness was comical, considering the long lecture she had given me. Being trustworthy was the most important thing I could do to gain respect. Being on time is a fundamental part of being trustworthy. I hadn't been late for anything yet, so I wasn't sure why she assumed I needed to hear this.

Del entered the bingo hall, trailing behind a lost-looking Lula while wearing the same Led Zeppelin shirt that he had worn the Sunday prior. He was trying to tell me something with his eyes. I have never been great at reading faces. Lula walked right past me and went around the room. She appeared to be taking it all in but also didn't seem normal. Del approached me and hovered forward with a whisper. I backed up almost immediately, as it was very clear he had conquered a bag of salt-and-vinegar chips.

"When I got to Lula's house, she wasn't ready to go." Del nodded in her direction.

"That's not like her."

"Well, it's more than that. She was confused about why I was there. She forgot we were coming today, and I had to remind her a few times what we were coming to do."

I tried to calm the situation. "Maybe I just gave her confusing information. I thought I had told her today. Maybe I wrote the wrong day down."

"No." Del looked slightly frustrated now. "It's more than that. I think she's got old timers."

CHAPTER 3:

Pomp and Circumstance

osling, 2020—It wasn't my fault that Gentry Lee was raised in the foster system. I did tell my Lula what I saw that day and then repeated it to the police and again in the courtroom, but there's no doubt in my mind that the man would have been caught on evidence alone. I can't be blamed. It wasn't a lie worth nursing.

Gentry and I crossed paths daily in school. Every time I saw him, the memory of his daddy festered in the forefront of my mind and reminded me daily that men are capable of the worst kind of evil.

He acted like he hated me for years after we met. But despite all that, I wanted him to know that I was sorry. I approached him in our eighth-grade science lab one day and sat down without being able to really look him in his eyes.

"Can we talk?" I asked him and then started to fiddle with the beaker in front of me.

Gentry looked puzzled that I was addressing him. He didn't say anything back.

I looked around the classroom. For some reason, when I talked to him, I didn't want to be noticed. No one really paid attention though. Jenny was passing a note to Franchesca, and a few other people looked like they were actually just doing the assignment.

Gentry ignored my question. His response was to take scissors to the back of my hair and cut out a chunk of my curls.

As I live and breathe, Gentry Lee held on to a misguided grudge like it was a sack full of two-dollar bills. I grew a grudge of my own, but I suppose his superseded mine. He couldn't have possibly assumed it was all my fault, but he was deeply disturbed by the situation and handled it in his way. I handled it in my own way as well.

I casually pretended Gentry wasn't in the room for years, all the way through to our tiny middle school graduation. I was in the top percentile of my middle school class, right along with Gentry. We both had a 4.0 grade point average. I couldn't wait until high school and felt so proud to be sitting on the stage with only the top twenty students.

I was ready for "pomp and circumstance." The first of many accolades well deserved. I made my way up to the stage; Gentry looked like he wanted to say something to me. Instead, as I passed his chair, he leaned his foot forward in attempt to trip me on the stage in front of the large crowd. He missed, thankfully, but I turned around and grabbed him by his tie and whispered real close to his face.

"You're just as terrible as your daddy, Gentry Lee."

I could tell the insult hit as hard as I wanted it to. He stared off into space the entire graduation and almost missed his name being called.

After that, Gentry didn't so much as shift his eyes in my direction until our third year of high school.

I didn't know much about the foster system, but it must not have been Gentry's cup of tea. I once heard him calling me spoiled and privileged to his group of raggedy jerk friends, but he didn't know enough about me to make that declaration. I had no parents. I might not have jumped from house to house, but I was not spoiled by any means.

His dad simply didn't try hard enough to not get caught. It was plainly a crime of passion, and he rode through town that day with the stench of murder escaping from his very pores. Tire tracks and boot tracks are what did him in, matched with a goodbye letter from Gentry's mama; it was basically an open-and-shut case. He shot the man who was having an affair with his mama, and it didn't take a genius to figure it out. Gentry's mama, on the other hand, died of a broken heart that day, leaving Gentry without parents.

He lived in Liberty long enough to graduate from high school and then left town.

I left town a few months after Gentry, at the end of the summer, and attended a college close enough to home that I could visit Lula monthly.

When my phone rang, I never would have expected Gentry's voice on the other end.

While I was in school, I started working with dementia patients and decided that I wanted to be there for the people who were left behind. I was never surprised by the lack of visitors for dementia patients. It is hard to see someone you love withering away, so many people decide just not to do it. I also understood that some people don't want to feel bad for their loved ones because they are harboring pain of their own.

I was in the middle of my morning shift at the Palm Village Retirement Community. Stephen Thompkins was refusing to shower again. He seemed to pick up some aversion to water shortly after he started living there. Stephen was my last patient of the morning. I checked off his medicine chart, did some light cleaning, and then started the thirty-minute routine of begging him to get into the shower.

Mr. Stephen was a few years into a dementia diagnosis. I could typically at least get him to change his drawers and socks, but lately even that had been a test of my endurance.

He was knee-deep in the paranoid stages of his disease and assured me daily that the nurses and staff were going to "get" him. He kept makeshift weapons on the couch by his side, such as frying pans and belts. I always moved them, but he was getting creative, and if a man wants to make a weapon, he will make it out of just about anything.

"Mr. Stephen, why do you have a tea kettle on your couch?"

He looked at me like I was dumb for asking. "In case I need to hit someone over the head with it."

At that point I figured I should probably get rid of the kettle and work with his family to possibly reevaluate his medication.

"Okay, Mr. Stephen, I see. Let's get you in the shower, and then after that, we will go get some ice cream in the lobby."

"No," he snarled. "They are going to kick me out if they see me with you. You are too young. I've heard them talking about me walking around with a young lady, but I haven't done anything. Did you see them? They are right outside my window looking at us now."

His blinds were wide open to an empty patio. I don't ever recommend lying to a patient with dementia. Usually it is best to take the conversation a different direction without confirming or denying what they are saying, depending on the situation.

Last time he was seeing men on his patio, it was due to a urinary tract infection. After the antibiotics and a Risperdal prescription, we were clear of hallucinations for a few months.

"Let's get you in the shower and work on getting you out of here, since you don't seem to like it much."

"You'd do that for me?" He seemed so sincere, like I was doing him a huge favor. Genuine fear struck his eyes and made his gray eyebrows stand at attention. I always wondered what Mr. Stephen was like when he was younger. There were pictures of him working on airplanes and dancing with his wife. He had a great sense of humor and joked often that it was the only sense he still had.

We typically started each visit listening to Elvis because it made him remember the favorite parts of his childhood, and he would light up and tell me about all the trouble he used to get into.

That was my favorite part of working with patients. Sometimes they would find themselves back in a moment, and I could tell that somehow, despite the disease, part of them was still brewing in there. Sometimes, however, they would realize that they were stuck behind the new person that the disease created. Those were always the most difficult moments.

"Let's get you in that shower so that you can be presentable."

Mr. Stephen walked into the bathroom willingly, but I knew he'd probably just stand at the counter while the water ran. It was in my job description to assist with his showers, but I needed to get rid of that teapot first.

Mr. Stephen disappeared into the bathroom, and I expected at least one or two visits from him before he took off his pants. He emerged almost immediately.

"What do I need to do?" he asked me with remorse on his face, understanding that he should know but didn't.

"I'll be right in. Just get undressed, and I'll help you with the next step," I said, thinking that should hold him over for a few seconds. Maybe.

I walked to the couch to pick up the teapot, but it felt heavy and full. Was he actually drinking out of it, or did he fill it up with water hoping it would cause more damage if he hit someone with it? No, there was too much logic involved for that to be the case. As I poured out the contents into the small kitchen sink, a foul odor overtook me. He had been peeing in the tea kettle.

I started gagging. Years in this career, and I've only gagged three times. Typically, I knew when to expect something gross. If I wasn't surprised, I could pretty much handle any and all bodily functions. Teapot urine wasn't anticipated.

I thought about Lula immediately. She'd sit on the porch with me after a long day at school and listen to every detail of my day while we drank a hot cup of tea with milk and sugar. She'd run her fingers through my wild tangles and listen to whatever school drama I had to share, and then we would sing songs into the night while she played the piano. I wasn't sure I'd ever look at tea the same way.

When Gentry called, he was calm. I thought maybe he was following through with the apology portion of a twelve-step program or something.

"Hi, Rosling. it's Gentry."

"Okay." I didn't know what else to say.

"I've moved back to Liberty. I'm going to be the pastor at your old church."

I thought he was joking. "I don't have a whole lot of time right now. I'm at work." I tried to end the conversation before it had a chance to start.

"Okay, this will not take long. I hope you're doing well. I'm here with your Lula." Oh Lord, he must have taken her hostage, I thought. "She seems to have forgotten where she lives, and I think you ought to come back to town to help sort out a few things for her."

"What do you mean she forgot where she lives?"

"She couldn't find her house this afternoon, and she didn't remember that we had a meeting scheduled. Different things like that."

Mr. Stephen emerged from the bathroom wearing just his underwear. "What the hell did you do with my teapot, woman?"

He lifted pillows and walked around the room in circles, not sure what to do with himself.

"Mr. Stephen, your pants are on the bed. Go ahead and get those on, and I'll be in to help you in just a minute."

"It sounds like I called at a bad time. I just thought you needed to know," said Gentry.

"Of course I need to know," I said.

"My pants?" Mr. Stephen was still in his underwear staring at me, waiting for the next step. His family would be walking through the door within the next ten minutes.

"I'll be there for Lula. Just give me a few days."

I hung up without saying goodbye and helped Mr. Stephen with his pants.

CHAPTER 4:

Old Wounds, Aged Scotch

Gentry, 2020—I have never told anyone that I saw my dad commit murder. The day I lost my Daddy was the same day I lost my Mama. Rosling headed in the direction of her home to a world of comfort while I ran home to find my mom lying on the floor in a pool of vomit. I'll never know whether she drank as much as she did with the intent of dying, but I looked into her dead eyes and knew I'd never get the answers to questions that were far more important than that one.

Daddy used to walk through rooms like the walls owed him something. He was charming, and he was strong. He provided for his family, and he never met a stranger. But he was also a broken man and tried to heal old wounds with aged scotch.

It's the same story that rings out behind closed doors across the world—Mama couldn't take it anymore. She met the most predictable man in the tri-county area, loved every boring detail about him, and decided that she was better safe than sorry. I thought again about unanswered questions. There is only one question that sticks with me. I'll never know whether she was going to take me with her.

I found my mom lying on the floor and dialed 911. Before I knew it, I was in a haze of sirens and questions.

When did I find her like this? Was there anyone else here? What time did she start drinking? Then the one that I knew the answer to. Where is your daddy?

I told them that Daddy left early that morning. Not a lie. I told them that Daddy usually started work around 5:00 a.m. and didn't get home until 3:00 p.m. Not a lie. I told them that I hadn't seen him in several hours. Technically not a lie.

Before I knew it, I was crying the kind of tears that seem to come from your eyes and your mouth. The messy kind of crying that holds your whole face hostage for days until you get every bit out.

Daddy must have seen the sirens because he didn't come home that afternoon. The police took me into the office to wait, and he never showed up there either. Once they found Mama's goodbye letter to Daddy, the pieces connected for them. The next morning, he was pulled over by the police three counties over.

I slept at the police station until about 4:00 a.m., when I was picked up by Anna Briggs, a social worker.

Anna had thick braids that came halfway down her back, and she was wearing jeans. I wondered why she wasn't dressed up for work. I guess with it being the middle of the night, she might have been woken up. She had a thick New Jersey accent and made me laugh even when it hurt.

I didn't have close remaining relatives to help plan a funeral for Mama. One of Mama's distant aunts arranged a meeting with a crematorium, and I sat in a wooden chair while they talked around me. Anna took me to Walmart to buy me a suit and made sure I had a nice boutonniere. Mama's aunt was in her late eighties and didn't feel up to the task of keeping me. She said the memorial was the least she could do. They put Mama's urn at the front of the church near the stage with two tall flowering plants and played nice music. A few people I recognized dropped in, but I didn't really know any of them well. A woman came through the door dressed in a black dress and a silver necklace. She walked up the aisle, but instead of approaching Mama's urn or the pastor to shake hands, she came to me.

"Are you Gentry?" she asked me.

"Yes."

She reached for my hand and held it for a minute while she cried. "I'm sorry. I never meant for this to happen."

She dropped my hand and began breathing heavy into a handkerchief.

"How did you know Mama?" I asked.

"I didn't." She walked away.

"What's your name?" I yelled at her back.

"Mae."

The day after the funeral, Anna walked me up to the front door of a two-story log cabin–style house. She patted my shoulder and smiled a little too enthusiastically while she talked about me like I wasn't in the room. I don't remember the names of the couple that took me in that first week. I just remember that they tiptoed around me like broken china on their hardwood floors. They constantly whispered and called me "buddy" as though they didn't remember my actual name. They bought four pairs of the same exact khaki pants. I didn't know what the holdup was on my actual clothes from home.

My first act of rebellion in the foster care system was to cut holes in the knees of all my new khakis and get them as dirty as possible.

Anna picked me up after a few nights with my temporary family.

The next few houses were a haze of temporary solutions. I wasn't dumb enough to get excited about the prospect of someone keeping a damaged preteen.

The worst part of all this was that I ran into Rosling at school almost daily. Every time I saw her, it reminded me of what I had seen in my daddy that day. It wasn't Rosling's fault, but for the better part of my life, I wanted to distance myself from her, and she knew it.

As the years went on, I felt a stronger pull to make things right with Rosling. It's a terrible thing to ask someone to hold on to a lie. I put Rosling in the worst possible position and then treated her like it was her fault.

Calling Rosling wasn't easy, but it had been my plan all along to make amends. I didn't think it would be under these circumstances. I thought Rosling would sound more surprised to hear from me. She was relatively quiet on the call. I delivered the information about her Lula and confirmed that she'd be returning to Liberty. She hung up without saying goodbye.

CHAPTER 5:

Let's All Be Ducks

Rosling, 2020—The doctor asked Lula the usual questions. She could tell him what year it was, her birthday, and so much more. He didn't ask for her Visa PIN, but she was ready to supply it if he was so inclined to ask.

Her short-term memory was the problem. The doctor said Lula was displaying early signs of Alzheimer's. I knew the day would come that I would need to take care of her. I looked forward to being able to give back to her what she had given me but hadn't realized it would be this soon.

As soon as the doctor gave his diagnosis, I informed my boss that I wouldn't be back to work. He understood and said I'd always have a job if I needed one. I lived in an apartment at the nursing home. He said he'd send my clothes and have housekeeping pack up the rest of my belongings for me to pick up whenever I was ready.

I don't know if Lula got herself ready that morning, but she was well put together in her burgundy blouse, black pants, leopard slip-on loafers, and leopard-framed glasses to match. Her gray hair had been color treated recently, and she was wearing black hoop earrings that seemed to tie the look together.

I realized at that moment that Lula could pull together a nice outfit with Alzheimer's, but it took me thirty minutes to find matching socks.

It was clear that Lula was in the earliest stages. She'd be forgetting her keys, getting lost in places that she didn't frequent often, and forgetting what she had come into the room for.

That would happen for a while. She'd likely tell me stories that she had already told me or ask me several times to reassure or remind her of things we had already talked about.

There was no great gauge of whether we were looking at months or years. I knew that I needed to prevent her from cooking or traveling, two things that are highly dangerous for Alzheimer's patients. Patients. Lula from here on out would be a patient.

Maybe she'd stop showering. Maybe she'd become paranoid. Maybe. There was no clear path, and no understanding of how either of us should proceed. Only time would tell.

We walked out of the doctor's office building to my car. Parked on the other side of the lot was a man wearing a black golf shirt, khakis, and a hat leaning against a very conspicuous blue 1976 Ford Mustang. He didn't break eye contact with me but didn't seem like he wanted to approach either. Maybe he was staring because I was staring, but it was odd, so I quickly got Lula in the car, and we drove toward her house.

When we arrived back home, I started the kettle. Thinking of Mr. Stephen all of a sudden, I had to power through it and continue making tea. Lula told me she'd invited Gentry to stop by. I was getting more nervous by the minute, knowing how we'd left things off the last time we saw each other in high school.

Earlier that day, I had walked through the new Target in town and purchased any baby-proofing gear I could find to protect her from turning on the stove, opening the oven, unsetting the alarm, walking out of the house at night, and so on.

I tried to get Lula to move to the guest bedroom downstairs so that she could avoid any fall risks. She pushed back hard on the suggestion and said there'd be no way she'd be away from her prayer closet each night. Her routine was her routine. I respected that for now, knowing that eventually we'd have to change it up.

I sat down with Lula for a moment and let my stupid thoughts exit my mouth. "Lula, you've always had it all together when I've been falling apart. I don't know how I'm gonna do it, but I promise you that I'm going to be here for you."

"I've always been a duck."

I thought maybe she'd taken an accelerated path down doolally tap lane and asked her what she meant.

"On the surface, I've been calm and collected to make sure you always felt safe. But under the surface, I've been paddling hard, baby."

I smiled at the analogy.

"All right, Lula. Let's all be ducks."

I was trying not to be nervous to see Gentry. We were both grown-ups. We both had careers, though his perplexed me. But when I saw him get out of his car, I was brought back to our final interaction in high school.

He was wearing blue jeans and a baseball cap that said IWU.

I walked onto the porch before Lula saw that he had arrived.

He spoke first. "Hey, Rosling."

I admittedly froze for a moment in the land of select-your-salutation. "Hi."

"It's been a long time. I know we probably have a lot of catching up to do, but I mainly wanted to come check on your Lula."

I couldn't say anything, and I just moved out of the way and held the screen door open so he could walk inside. He visited her for about ten minutes and then told me he'd catch up with me soon as he walked out the door.

CHAPTER 6:

Lion's Den

entry, 2020—It was my first time seeing Rosling in years. She had always been pretty. She had wild hair and soulful, green eyes that tugged you in if you dared look in their direction. I made sure to do that as little as possible while we were growing up.

I feigned the correct things to say to her, visited Lula for a much shorter period of time than I had intended, and then disappeared into the car after telling Rosling that we'd "catch up."

We had nothing to catch up on. See any murders lately? What was I thinking?

She brushed me off and didn't take me seriously. I understood why.

A few weeks ago, before Lula started showing symptoms of memory loss, she drove me past the old church property. She asked me if I'd ever been inside it.

"Once or twice as a kid. With my mom," I said.

"Gentry, I know you were dealt a tough hand as a kid, and I know that you saw things as a child that nobody should ever have to see. You're going into the lion's den.

Like Daniel. It's not going to be easy. But this town needs it. You're obviously a man of great faith now, but you've got to show the people of this church that they can count on you as a leader."

"I understand that, Lula. That's why I'm here."

"Have you ever been taken to the prison to see your daddy?"

"I haven't seen him since I was ten years old," I said.

"Would you ever want to?"

I wanted to see him, but I wasn't ready. "I don't know."

Lula saw my discomfort and changed the subject. "I want you to know something else."

"What's that?"

"I want you to know that I've got your back. If they give you any trouble at all, I've got your back. If they all decide to stop coming to service, I've got your back. Because I see it in you. I see that you truly are a disciple and a disciple maker. You're on the right team. Therefore, we're in this together."

Lula was already my favorite person.

"There's a few people who will definitely have some issues with me being here."

"You mean Mae?"

"Well, her too, yes. Mostly I mean Rosling."

"Ah, you let me handle her." She patted me on the wrist before we went to lunch to talk about the future of the church. "One more thing," she said. "I'm in charge."

I smiled and nodded. "Noted."

CHAPTER 7:

Mac Landry

Lula, 1967—Mac was six foot three with sandy-blond hair and deep green eyes. He could dance a hole through concrete. Mac was the best year of my life. If his first love hadn't been the air force, he'd likely still be alive.

Rosling got her green eyes and blond curls from Mac's side of the family, and Rosling's mama had them too.

Mac Landry, a legend, came into town while I was working as a secretary.

We frequented the same restaurant for lunch for months before I even realized it. He hadn't changed out of his uniform yet, which automatically discredited him. I was so used to seeing military men float through town banking on finding themselves a temporary romance, and I made up my mind just staring at the back of his head while I waited in line behind him.

He had no idea that he had already lost points but made things worse for himself when he turned around and spilled Coke on my new floral dress. He offered his sincere apologies, and I tried to show him the door.

He followed me out of the restaurant and offered to buy me a new dress if I needed one, holding out a few bucks and reaching into his socks for quarters. I told him I could wash clothes just fine and that he was making a presumptuous offer. He was certainly cute in his attempts, however.

"You're awfully frustrated. I can see this. Is there any possible way at all that I can make this up to you?"

"I don't know," I said. I turned to walk away from him.

"At least tell me your name," he said.

"Lula."

"Lula, what's your surname?" he asked, trying to get me to stay longer.

"I'm Lula Belle Rosling."

He smiled. "Is there any way that we can talk just a little longer, Lula Belle Rosling?"

I told him to come to my parents' house that evening for dinner. He joined us that evening and ate real barbeque for the first time. His appetite brought him back for dinner several times over the next two weeks. Each night after eating, we'd play gin rummy on the porch until midnight. He said that if I wasn't interested in his attempts at courtship, I'd have to stop giving him reasons to fall in love with me.

It didn't take long to realize that he was the one for me. Since he was a military man, I was worried I'd have to eventually leave Liberty, but I would have gone to Mars for him.

My lace wedding dress hung patiently next to his suit. Flowers and songs were selected, and he found his way into the hearts of my parents. He didn't have any parents, and mine were past the age of retirement. Every detail of our wedding was planned out. We'd be married in my backyard. I just couldn't wait to become Lula Landry.

"Yes" was the easiest word I'd ever uttered. The vows escaped my tongue and floated up to the sky, glittered with lightning bugs who came out that night just for us.

We danced into a burning sunset and then danced on through the next six months until he got his orders. It was time to go. Vietnam. The next few weeks felt like a blur. My parents passed away. I learned I was pregnant and then a few months later received word that Mac had died in Vietnam. My parents left me the house on Liberty Creek. I was twenty-eight years old and pregnant with the only child I'd ever have.

I started having contractions at 9:15 a.m. on a Sunday morning during the church service. Reverend Little had already started his sermon after a few hymns.

I was sitting behind a structural column next to a family of four. I thought I might try to hold off on leaving, and I didn't want to make a scene, but pain kicked in. Many in the congregation must have thought that I was really feeling the Holy Spirit, because I got to moaning, and every time I made a sound, the room would erupt in agreement. I realized I needed to get out of the church, so I pushed past the people sitting next to me and stood in the aisle. I tried to waddle in the direction of the side door right at the time Pastor finished prayer and invited people to the front for altar call.

"No, no, no," I tried to say as several people moved their way up to the front of the church, one lady grabbing me by the arm, trying her best to be helpful to the poor pregnant lady who just wanted to make it up to the front.

Reverend Little walked over to me and squeezed my shoulders as he prayed. "Lord Jesus, we pray for Lula Landry and this baby. Let the rest of her pregnancy be well, Lord, and keep her and the baby safe in your hands."

In the midst of hallelujahs and heavy prayer, my water broke right atop the foot of Reverend Little.

His eyes looked up in shock, but he handled it well.

Not many people get a fifteen-car caravan to the hospital when they have a baby. But the Lord and his people all decided to show up that day. Reverend Little and the congregation stayed in the waiting room for the three hours that I pushed.

Baby girl finally blessed me with her presence. She looked like her father and had all ten fingers and toes to boot.

They cut the cord and moved around me rhythmically, sewing this and cutting that until someone came in and asked me what I was going to name the baby girl.

"Mac. Mac Landry, just like her daddy."

CHAPTER 8:

The Promises in Our Teacups

Rosling, 2020—Lula announced that lunch was ready. We walked to the front porch and sat down at the table together. We ate silently for a few minutes until Lula finished her sandwich.

"Lula, do you ever have questions about God? Do you always have faith?"

"Rosling, I always have questions, but I also always have faith," she said.

I felt like I'd never understand.

"It's like this," she said. "You can have all these things that you don't understand but still believe that God's working everything for the good of those who love him. There's this verse in the Bible that if we have faith the size of a mustard seed, we can move mountains."

I needed a change of subject because I didn't want to reveal to Lula that I wasn't on the same page. "With everything that's going on, is there anything you're worried about? You know, anything you want me to make sure of?"

"I'm not going to be able to play piano anymore."

"Lula, you might still be able to play for a long time. It can take years before you hit the next stages."

"Rosling, I don't know how long I'm going to be lucid enough to say this to you." Lula grabbed onto my hand. "I'm not going to waste any time. The only community I've ever been a part of is that church. Raising your mama and then raising you. It's the only family I've had for close to fifty years. We've lost our pastor, we've lost our sanctuary, and now the church is one step closer to losing me. There needs to be a light at the end of the tunnel. They need to see new life and new progress."

I wanted to help, but short of making pies, I didn't know how to help or in what capacity she wanted me to serve.

I had promised myself a long time ago I would never break Lula's heart, which was the exact reason that I didn't want her to know I didn't share her belief system. I was not a Christian. From the time I was a baby, Lula brought me to church. I never had a chance to decide for myself, and half the time I didn't understand a thing that the preacher man was saying. The day I saw the murder, it became harder and harder for me to accept that there was a God who wouldn't stop such a terrible thing from happening.

Gentry Lee stepping up to the pulpit made me wonder whether the credentials for preaching the gospel were getting more and more lax as time went on.

I thought for a moment that Gentry might have become a pastor at Lula's church just to make my life miserable. I laughed a little at the thought of Gentry talking about the Ten Commandments. Don't lie, don't cheat, and don't steal. The Gentry I knew was in the business of breaking those rules, not preaching them. I started giggling out loud, and Lula looked at me like I was the one losing my mind.

"Okay, Lula. I'm here to help. What can I do? Didn't you always have a big lunch at the church?"

"Piano. You can play the piano?"

"Piano?" I didn't know how to play piano or any other instrument.

"I'm going to teach you to play the piano while I'm still able minded enough to do it. And I won't take no for an answer."

"Okay," I said. "It would be nice to learn how to play, actually. I'll do it."

"Good. That's settled then. About those lunches, they don't need to be here. In fact, Mae has basically taken them over, and Gentry said we had a space for them at the new church building," she said.

"Okay, well, that lightens things a bit," I said, grateful that I wouldn't need to clean the house afterward.

"You should still make something, though. Any dessert or side dish is fine usually. But no nuts."

I laughed when I thought about the people in the town. *Everyone in this town is nuts. There goes the entire guest list.*

"We have several people with nut allergies." Lula explained.

"Any aversions to gluten?" I smirked.

"Not that I know of. You're in the south. Gluten is part of these people's biological makeup, but you can confirm when we meet with Pastor Gentry."

43

"Why do I need to deal with Gentry?" I looked at her with my best "don't make me do it" face.

"Cause he's the pastor, Rosling. What on earth? He doesn't have cooties anymore, if that's what you're worried about."

I didn't sign up for this.

CHAPTER 9:

Middle C

osling, 2020—"This is middle C."

Lula held her thumb, middle finger, and pinky on the three piano keys to show me where to start. She didn't want to teach me to read music yet and said that learning chords would be the best bet because it was faster.

Lula had tried to teach me to play piano when I was younger, but I never sat still long enough to take the information in. I'd fiddle around at the bench and make as much noise as possible until she got tired of trying.

The old wooden piano sat in the front sitting room of her house. Recently, Lula had hung a painted canvas of the creek on the wall above it in a gold frame. The piano was adjacent to the only interior wall in the front sitting room, and at the other end of the room was a large window that spanned the entire wall. I often sat on the white sofa in front of that window reading while Lula played. She'd recently added multiple accent pillows of various colors and a refurbished teal coffee table.

"I am going to teach you the major and minor chords first, and then, before you know it, you'll be able to do this."

Each hand moved around while her foot jumped up and down on the sustain pedal. She was playing "Spirit in the Sky."

"Really, Lula." I smiled, knowing there was more classic rock where that came from.

"Follow me with C, D, E, F, G, then A and B. Watch my hands, but mostly for now my right hand. Once you master where everything is, you'll be able to jump from one chord to the next."

"When do I learn how to play with my foot?" I asked.

She smiled at me before shaking her head. "First, you'll learn the basics of playing with the right hand, then I'll teach you how to simultaneously play with the left hand, and then your feet."

"Why are there three foot pedals?"

"Whoa, you're getting way ahead of yourself. Slow down. There are more chords, and you'll be able to play fancy like me over time, but to start you just need to be able to stay in the right chord at the right time. Ready?"

I was ready to do whatever she needed. For eighteen years I had fallen asleep to her playing piano.

Each Saturday, Lula would make us a huge dinner for whatever company we would have. She'd prepare a roast or something else elaborate as I sat at the kitchen counter watching her intently. She'd put on Motown and dance around, singing into a spoon as she told me to pour and stir. Music brought her to life.

When music was not playing, Lula was playing music. Her hips swung faster than a mixer in cake batter.

"I know you want to leave me, but I refuse to let you go. If I had to beg, plea, for your sympathy, I don't mind, 'cause you mean that much to me."

She sang it loud and then gave me a history lesson on Motown. It was magical to watch someone who was always so composed let loose to words that had so much soul. She brought me up on every genre of music, from the Temptations to the hymns of Charles Wesley.

After every meal, I'd help clean up, and we would sit on the porch until the sun went down. Scents of whatever we cooked would linger in the house as I laid my head down, and she'd sing out into the night for hours. Sometimes I tried to stay awake and listen, but typically sleep overtook me long before she turned in.

Now as we sat at the piano, I was wholeheartedly ready to learn. Not for myself and not for a faith that I wasn't sure I had, but because I needed her music. If I could hold onto that piece of Lula, I knew I'd have some of her goodness inside of me forever.

"We're learning 'It Is Well with My Soul' next week," Lula said as she handed me a sheet of music.

Lula got up from the piano bench and told me to practice moving my right hand from C to D, and then from D to E until I was able to move through all chords seamlessly.

"I'm going to make us some tea," said Lula.

She walked into the kitchen while my hands moved around the piano. I wondered how long it would take for muscle memory to kick in because overall it felt awkward, and my thumb continued to slam down on the wrong key while the others held up their end of the lesson.

I could hear Lula moving around the kitchen, and then she passed me again to head upstairs.

She yelled on her way up, "Don't hit the keys like they've done you wrong, Rosling."

Minutes passed, and the tea kettle was whistling, so I walked into the kitchen to finish up making the tea. Each cup was ready and sitting on the counter. Lula walked back into the kitchen.

"I'm going to make us some tea," she announced it again. The two cups of tea sat directly in front of the kettle, but still she filled the kettle with water and placed it on its burner.

"Lula, I've made some. I went ahead and finished them up while you went upstairs."

"What do you need from upstairs?" she asked me.

"I don't need anything from upstairs. You just went upstairs while I made the tea."

It took her a few seconds to be in her own head, and then she nodded and turned around to get new teacups out. This was the first I had seen of her Alzheimer's since being back in town. The behavior was minor, definitely early stages, but enough to jolt me into a reality I wasn't ready for. Before I could feel any emotion about it, she returned to the moment.

"Oh, you already made some. Are you trying to avoid practicing? You'll never learn if you don't get back in there. Next time just let me get the tea."

She smiled like I was trying to put one past her. It reminded me of when I was a kid.

After a few hours of practicing, I could already move my right hand around the chords. But I still wasn't sure whether I was hitting majors or minors.

"Okay, Rosling." She sat back at the bench. "Next is your left hand. You are going to start over here just hitting one at a time while you jump with your right hand. So if you are hitting the C chord, your pinky should hit this C over here simultaneously."

It made sense, and I caught on to that quickly as well.

By Saturday evening, I could jump my right hand around to basic chords and properly jump my foot on and off the sustain pedal at the proper time. Well, mostly.

"There are more chords that you will need to learn over time, but we will start on those next week." Lula's affirmation that I was doing well was exciting.

CHAPTER 10:

Uncomfortable

Gentry, 2020—Rosling and Lula sat in front of me at a small sandwich shop with faces full of expectation. Lula did most of the talking while Rosling sipped her coffee. I've never known two people to drink more caffeine.

"I will play the keys for the next few months but will also be teaching Rosling so that she can take over when I can no longer play," Lula said.

Rosling looked at her grandmother frequently as we spoke. It was endearing.

Lula seemed to have it all planned out. Neither of them knew what exactly would happen or when.

"We should recruit more musicians," I said.

"You mean you'd audition anyone off the street even if they aren't part of the church?" Lula looked curious.

"Well, I know it's not ideal, but that's one way to start a conversation about Jesus," I said. "The entire point is to bring the sheep into the pasture, not lock them out because they aren't members."

Rosling looked up at me from her coffee. I couldn't read her expression, but I knew she hadn't expected me to say that.

Lula snapped back, "I know that you think you are different now, but that doesn't mean that all people in the world are good or even capable of becoming good."

"I don't think I'm different now," I said. "I know that I am different now. And that happened because I surrounded myself with people who welcomed me instead of judging me. If that hadn't happened, I'd probably have a random degree and no sense of direction."

"I agree with him," Rosling said, and we made eye contact. "Don't get me wrong. I am going to learn how to play the piano, but I think you may want to consider inviting new people to the church anyway."

"We invite people all the time." Lula was irritated.

"No, I mean people who..." Rosling stopped and didn't finish her sentence. I knew where she was going with it though.

"Every person in the congregation is there because they already have a relationship with Jesus," Gentry went on.

"Well, of course they do. That's why they are in church." Lula looked at him like he was an idiot.

"Some percentage of the church building should consist of people who are just finding their way through the doors. Broken people. People who need to learn more about Jesus. Honestly, if everyone is remaining in their comfort zones, we aren't doing it right."

"Well, Rev—" Lula chuckled with a gleam in her eye— "you certainly know how to make a roomful of Christians uncomfortable." She laughed at herself, proud of the comment. "You better hurry up and finish up restoring that bingo hall, because Mae Whitlow is not going to have a bunch of miscreants sitting in her parlor, even if Jesus himself told her to."

CHAPTER 11:

Mae you live happily ever after

Mae, *1995*—"I don't like the spicy jelly beans," said Lenny. Her blond curls bounced while she walked up the sidewalk.

"Candy isn't spicy, Lenny. Do you mean sour?"

I laughed at her little disposition. She was cute as a drawer full of purple buttons and all mine for the day.

My husband Bill and I hadn't had our own kids yet, so I borrowed our neighbor's daughter to babysit as often as I could. I knew what I wanted early in life. I was the little girl who played with dolls and didn't have an interest in going to college. I wanted to be a mommy, and I had wanted it to happen for as long as I could remember.

I would be the best mommy in the world to a little girl. There was nothing in the world that I'd be better at, in fact. However, I would have taken a son as long as he turned out like Bill.

Bill was such a hard worker, always attentive to his boss and quick to work overtime. He kept taking care of me. We married right after high school, and I knew that it was only a matter of time before he'd let us try for a baby.

Lenny was mine several times a week while her mother took some time to herself. We'd walk around town, and I'd buy lunch and treats and typically spoil her with clothes and whatever else she asked for.

She was a sweet child. She loved spending time with me, and I couldn't help but think that one day I'd get one just like her. I'd be there to console her when her friends weren't up to snuff, and I'd teach her how to be a good person. I'd love that child with every fiber of my being, and there'd be nothing in the universe that could stop me from being the best mother that ever lived.

About a year ago, I asked Bill to take me to my yearly lady physical. Bill sat in the waiting room while I met with the doctor and talked about my ovulation schedules and my last period. He took note that it had been over a month since my last period.

I was giddy. I couldn't wait to tell Bill. A baby. Finally a baby.

I nearly ran out to the waiting room with my face flushed in a pure fit of excitement. He stood up quickly, ready to get out of the waiting area, I suppose, and we walked to the car. As soon as I was buckled, I told him he was going to be a daddy.

"We've got an ultrasound in a week," I said.

We were back in the doctor's office to get the ultrasound. Bill insisted on sitting in the waiting room instead of coming in to the room with me.

I lay on the table with my gown hiked up, and the ultrasound technician told me that it would be cold. No hand to hold, so I just crossed them on my chest and held my own hands. She wiggled that thing around without comment long enough for me to know something was wrong.

"I can't be certain. I see the egg, but this is not what we would expect to see right now. Let's get you back to see the doctor."

A blighted ovum, they said. I'm no college graduate, but I know enough to understand that it wasn't good.

The doctor gave me options.

"You can either have the procedure to remove it, or it will pass on its own. There are some dangers to letting it pass on its own, however."

There was no way I was going to have them take it out if it had a chance of becoming anything viable.

I was naturally inconsolable. The doctor asked me if I wanted to walk out the back door so I wouldn't have to go through the waiting area. I'm thinking he was worried I might scare off some of his real patients.

Bill knew it was the worst news I had ever received, but he barely shrugged.

The doctor said I'd probably go on to have children after this. It's far more common than people realize.

He also told me that waiting for my blighted ovum to pass naturally would be only mild discomfort. Like a bad menstrual cramp. He was wrong about that too.

I went on from there to have two other pregnancies, both ending in miscarriages in the first trimester. Bill began working later. I started attending church, where I served weekly in the nursery, and I was also spending as much time as possible babysitting and helping other people care for their children when needed.

This particular Tuesday, Lenny and I went shopping the next town over. We were walking toward a little café to grab a bite to eat. Lenny had been talking about a hot dog since the second she hopped into the car that morning.

As I neared the window, I saw a familiar face. There sat Bill. He must have been on a lunch with a client, I thought. He was eating a basket of fries and had two Cokes in front of him on the table.

I waved really big from the window, but he didn't see me. I noticed the Cokes were both on his side of the table. A woman came and sat down right next to him, and he kissed her square on the mouth before wrapping his arms around her.

I walked into that café with Lenny and stood in front of him and his friend, smiling cordially.

"Hi, Bill. I don't get to usually see you during your workday, honey."

He moved farther away from the woman and looked very uncomfortable, as he should have.

"I'm making your favorite dinner tonight, so don't fill up too much on stuff that's bad for you." I nodded at the woman and turned with Lenny to walk out of the café.

Bill didn't address the situation when he got home. He walked right into his office and closed the door behind him. If I couldn't scare him into being a good person, I'd have to find someone who would.

The day I approached David Lee, I knew I was playing with fire.

I dug for days to figure out who the woman was, and I learned she was also married—with a ten-year-old son to boot.

I casually drove into his auto shop and told him that my tire alignment seemed off.

After he looked at the car and charged me a fair amount to confirm nothing was in fact wrong with it, I asked him if he knew what his wife had been getting up to.

He was good looking enough. I wasn't sure why his wife would be stepping out. He had dark eyes and hair that swooped to the side of his forehead. Beautiful bone structure, and he looked quite fit. One feature I didn't care for, as I am not a fan of tattoos, was the catfish that peered out from his shirt sleeve and seemed to be swimming down his forearm. To others that might have been an even bigger selling point.

I let him know what I had seen in the café that day, and he quietly nodded and continued to twist the dry dirty towel that was in his hands.

I let him know that my husband didn't seem fazed by me finding out, and I'd like it if someone else could politely remind him that the institution of marriage is sacred.

"I can take care of this." He said it with no emotion and placed his towel down on a shelf.

By "take care of it," I assumed he meant he was going to break them up, accuse his wife, maybe even rough up Bill enough to set him straight for a while. I didn't know that he'd kill him.

Bill didn't leave for work the next morning like he normally did. He said he felt ill and needed to do some thinking. I didn't bother making him a lunch, but I did kiss him goodbye. He looked at me sweetly and kissed my temple.

"Mae Whitlow, I don't know what came over me. I'm going to make it up to you."

I walked out the door, and that was the last time I saw him.

Bill and I were high school sweethearts. We spent many Friday nights going to football games, dances, parties, and in general just cutting up. When we got married, something fizzled out, but I always knew we were capable of getting it back. I would have stayed with him forever. I would have gone on with him as my quiet husband, never having any children if that meant that we could keep being Bill and Mae. There was a different plan and a different set of circumstances.

This was a pain that would never go away. Every hope and dream that I ever had crashed down in a matter of months. There would be no babies. There would be no more Bill. I was on my own, and it forever changed who I was.

CHAPTER 12:

The House of the Mae

Rosling 2020—Sunday morning, I parked at the far end of Mae Whitlow's driveway under a Spanish oak. I figured it would yield more shade and allow for a cooler car when it was time to go. I pulled the keyboard out of the trunk and tried to simultaneously balance a peach pie as I walked up to the front of the house so that Lula and the band could begin practicing before everyone else arrived.

I had put on a casual dress with black ballet flats and pulled my curly hair back into the neatest braid I could muster. Lula always told me that my "Sunday best" was secondary to the sweet glow that came from my pure heart. Every time she'd say it, I blushed in shame, reminding myself that I could never really be who she thought I was.

"Lula Belle Landry." Mae said it like she was in trouble. "You cannot stick me alone in the room with that convict anymore. I cannot control my tongue, and he will drive me to sin."

I wondered what Gentry had done to ruffle her feathers already. It was only eight in the morning.

"Well, he is your pastor, Mae. And by the way, his daddy is the convict, not him."

"You tell that to my lawn equipment. Once a criminal, always a criminal."

"Now Mae..." Lula shot a snarky and comical glance her way. "You wanna tell me you've never committed a crime? You were basically a legend, Mae Whitlow. Didn't you and a certain late husband of yours once streak across the football field in your high school days? Last I heard, public nudity is against the law."

"That's gossip." She turned on her heel after scoffing at Lula and walked back into her house. We followed her in to investigate the cause of the altercation.

"What seems to be the problem, Gentry?" Lula asked him as though she was bored with his answer before he gave it.

"Oh, there's no problem. Mae is not quite happy with the playlist this week, but it's going to be just fine."

"Not one hymn," Mae yelled out from the kitchen.

"Mae, what are you doing in the kitchen?" Lula yelled from the parlor.

"Staring intently at my appliances while the faith of our congregation hangs in the balance of a vagabond. He's wearing jeans, Lula. Jeans."

"Well, as long as you are in there, can you make us some tea and coffee?" Lula rarely found herself pulled into useless altercations.

I looked up at Gentry, who indeed was wearing jeans, a button-down shirt, and nice brown shoes. He looked okay to me. Gentry glanced my way with a kind smile.

As the band practiced, I watched Lula's hands jump around the keyboard to the songs for the week. Until that day, I had never pictured music in my head as it played. For each part of the song, I knew where her hands would land on the keyboard and felt more confident about the sheet of lyrics and chords that rested on the stand of her keyboard.

"Okay, everyone, we're still waiting on Del, so we can pause practice for a few minutes," said Gentry.

In perfect timing, a 2000 Honda with missing hubcaps could be spotted rolling into the driveway.

"I knew he wouldn't be too late," said Gentry.

Lula lifted one blind—a narrow space to pass narrow judgment.

"Does that boy shower?"

"I'm sure he does. He smells like fresh laundry." Gentry laughed at himself, but Lula wasn't amused.

"Filthy or not, that boy loves Jesus," Lula decided.

Gentry's smile grew, and he nodded into his guitar case.

Del entered the house and started apologizing. "I didn't want to be late. I was watching my baby sister for Mom. There's a chance I may need to bring her to a few practices, and maybe when we renovate. Will that be okay?"

"Absolutely. We'll get the nursery as ready and clean as possible so that she can nap in there while we work. We can even see if any of the normal nursery volunteers can help during those times. Just let me know."

"Thanks, Pastor Gentry."

It was time to continue practicing.

"Who is playing the drums?" Mae's eyebrows disapproved of Gentry's confirmation that Del would be leading drums that week. Gentry would be on guitar and Lula on the keys.

"Well, who's singing?" She moved her head forward and then angled it to remove any possibility of confusion about the fact that she did not like Gentry.

Gentry confirmed that he would be signing, and Mae ushered us all to the back patio to set up our instruments and sound check. She had more than fifty chairs lined up under a tent from the previous Sunday's service like there would be a wedding.

After practice, while we were breaking everything down, Mae approached Gentry.

"You don't plan on stealing anything today, right?" she asked pointedly, raising her eyebrows at him while she shuffled through the room.

"No, I've already committed a felony today, so I'm taking a few hours off."

Gentry might not have been earning points with Mae Whitlow, but I certainly appreciated the comedic relief.

CHAPTER 13:

Homecoming

Rosling, 2002—I could hear the limo pull into Lula's driveway. Mostly I could hear the sounds of my best friends getting out of it. I was not quite ready, but I would have stayed up in my room analyzing my appearance forever if nobody gave me a timeline. My dress would easily have looked beautiful on any of my friends. My blue sequined dress hung on me like I was just a hanger, storing it in the closet. Lula had to alter the thing everywhere and then still had to pin it the day of.

My hair was supposed to be an updo with curly bits coming down in the front, but the stylist never gave me the curly bits. Just a high blob of curly hair, which I already rocked daily.

I quickly looked out the window to see a crowd of chiffon and corsages making their way to the door. Lula would be ready with the camera, and we'd drive off to eat at the nicest restaurant near our county, Verbena on Main. My plan was to order some kind of seafood pasta and a Coke. I was honestly more interested in dinner than I was my date.

I managed to run down the hardwood stairs in high-heeled shoes, which should be an Olympic sport. I wasn't in charge of booking the limos. My friends just arranged me a date because I still didn't have one the two weeks prior. They said it was junior homecoming, for crying out loud.

We always picked Lula's house for pictures because it had a scenic background with the creek edging up to the backyard. I laughed when I saw how big the crowd of teens was. My friends were overdoing it this time. I counted eight couples, mostly the usual suspects, and then my eyes landed on Gentry.

"Kennedy." I pulled my friend aside and tugged at her arm. "What is he doing here?"

"Gentry? Oh. It's weird, right? He doesn't talk to anybody usually. Well, Erin asked him to be her date. I mean, me and Erin just recently became friends again, so I hadn't talked to her a lot about who she was bringing."

My face sank, and I got a pit in my stomach.

"Is this okay? Do you hate him or something? Or worse, do you like him?"

I laughed and playfully smacked Kennedy on the arm. "No. neither. He's just...weird."

"Yah. But Erin's my friend, okay, so don't you be weird too."

I smiled. "Wouldn't dream of it."

We all huddled around to take pictures in the backyard, switching places while Lula pretended to be a professional. Gentry didn't cut his eyes in my direction once, at least not that I saw. Though my focus remained steady on him for most of the time.

The limos caravanned to Verbena on Main. My date had already taken interest in someone else's date. He promised to still dance with me and buy my dinner but asked if he could sit next to her. I didn't care.

Kennedy's boyfriend James dressed in a suit that was far too expensive for someone in high school; he looked like he was attending his wedding. He was putting on the charm too. He pulled out Kennedy's chair and then mine, then reached for Erin's chair as well. The three of us sat together with Gentry and James across from us. My date was off having a great time with someone else at a different table.

The server came by several times, and our table just couldn't get it together. I knew exactly what I wanted. The seafood pasta with shrimp, lobster, and crab meat. Sign me up. Eventually the rest of them ordered—with rather boring decisions, I might add—and we reached the short window of time when the food is prepared.

The restaurant had white tablecloths and lit candles on each table. Our group was eating inside, but the patio outside overlooked a beautiful stream with a rock wall reaching up to the stars.

I ate enthusiastically while the rest of the table tried to be as proper as possible. Erin and Kennedy ran off to the bathroom after they finished to check their teeth and makeup. James got up to go make his rounds and be the social butterfly he was. I wondered if anyone else noticed that James's ego walked into rooms before he did.

It was just Gentry and me at the table, and I was staring down at my lap avoiding conversation at all costs.

"You look really pretty tonight."

Why did he say that? What was his angle?

"Thanks. You don't have to be nice to me. In fact, it confuses me when you're nice to me, so please don't be nice to me."

"Would you rather me be mean to you?" He said it deadpan. Then he started looking around as though he was curious if anyone was coming back.

"I'd rather just not know you."

"You and everyone else," he said. That was a heavy statement to make. I never realized how true that probably was.

Gentry was dressed in a dark-blue suit with a light-gray tie. I could tell he had a fresh haircut.

"You look nice too."

"Thank you." He didn't look in my direction but smiled and nodded.

We ate and paid, my date making true on his promise to purchase my meal. Then we got back into the limos into the direction of the dance. The people from our table were the same ones who got into our particular limo: James, Kennedy, Gentry, Erin, and me. I didn't mind being the fifth wheel.

At the dance, I avoided Gentry and many others and tried to float around to compliment the nicest people I could find. I didn't do much dancing, but I did a lot of talking. Occasionally I could see Gentry glancing my way and smiling kindly.

James must have found a way to spike the punch or bring in his own loot because he spent his time in the bathroom throwing up while Kennedy was brought onstage for homecoming court. She didn't win, but she looked beautiful up there in her silver dress.

It was time to go. My same skimpy group piled into the limo, and I was supposed to be dropped off first. James, drunk, began banging on the limo driver's window, demanding he pull over. He had to throw up again.

He made it out in time and threw up on the side of the road. Kennedy got out to check on him, and he exploded into a person we hadn't seen before.

"I don't need your help, Kennedy. You aren't my mother."

"I'm not trying to be your mom. I just wanted to help."

"Get back in the limo."

Kennedy didn't know better and foolishly started arguing with him while he hovered over his own vomit.

"You're so mean, James. So mean. I wish I had never started dating you."

He paused long enough to insult her, and I could see Gentry starting to become very uncomfortable, like he visibly wanted to insert himself into their fight.

"You're a tease. And honestly not a pretty one. I can do way better, and it will probably be with someone who actually puts out." He spit onto the concrete.

Gentry got out of the limo and approached him quickly with a purpose.

"Stop, Gentry. What are you doing?" I pleaded from the car. Erin and I sat across from each other. She cried. I watched.

"If you ever talk to her or any other girl like that again within ear reach of me, I'll knock you out. Do you hear me?" I realized that Gentry's hand was around James' throat.

I got out of the limo to approach just as James's fist went back to punch Gentry. He came close to hitting me instead, but hit Gentry in the eye. Gentry tackled him while Kennedy and I yelled in protest. The limo driver got out and finally broke them up. James had to sit up front while we rode home in silence. I continued to look across at Gentry, who refused to make eye contact with anyone.

Growing up, I'd heard plenty of stories about the way Gentry's dad treated his mom. I wondered if Gentry was thinking about her.

CHAPTER 14:

Straight to the Fire

Mae, 2020—After Bill died, I gave my life to the church. I expanded the nursery and youth programs, and I never said no to a chance to help in any capacity. It became my reason for existing.

When Bill passed, I was the recipient of two forms of life insurance: one from his company and one that we paid for individually. Bill was nothing if not practical. Our home and car were paid off already. I was also paid a small amount from my work in the church office, but with what Bill left me, I wanted for nothing.

No one else served as willingly or diligently as I did. When Reverend Little had his heart attack, I took over teaching every Sunday. I wasn't much for preaching, but we all met and had Bible study and listened to music. We made it a point to continue meeting in his absence, and I arranged for other local pastors to rotate visiting to give sermons.

The day of the phone call, I was doing heavy cleaning around the office building that attached to the large brick sanctuary. The blinds were in dire need of cleaning, and

I was tired of the musty smell. I was certain that the office hadn't been cleaned since before we lost Reverend Little. When he was around, there were five of us who worked thirty hours a week in that office. Once he passed, it eventually trickled down to just me and a few volunteers each week. I was the only one, it seemed, who was organized and clean enough to file things appropriately and clean up after a hard workweek. I took out the trash, cleaned the blinds, dusted, and mopped. Then I refreshed the bathrooms with bleach. There was a heavy bleach smell, so I opened the windows and lit a few freesia candles to try masking one strong smell with another strong smell.

I got the call early afternoon from the district saying that they had found a new pastor to send out. I was ready to train him up and show him our church and community. I was ready to bring him in and help him learn the ropes, so to speak. It would be a great addition to a thriving church. We needed fresh eyes, and I was excited for what was coming. I was ready.

When they asked whether the name Gentry Lee meant anything to me, I almost spit out my coffee. The name meant too much to me.

When they gave me Gentry's name as the new reverend, I was overwhelmed. I felt quite sick, actually. I packed up my car, locked up the building, and failed to blow out the candles.

In my life I've done right, and I've done wrong. But I never meant to leave those candles lit. I never meant for any of this to happen.

None of it surprised me. This man's family had already burned up the rest of my world. Gentry's return to town just finished the job.

I couldn't fathom how a boy of his circumstances could be placed in charge of leading our church back to a viable condition.

"They must be letting anyone be a reverend these days!" I said out loud as I drove home angry. Unbeknownst to me, the church was in flames. I knew it was figuratively, but I didn't know that it was literally.

It was all my fault.

As soon as I remembered the candles, I sped back to see smoke filling the sky.

I stood in front of the firefighters and officers and cried, pleading for them to not take me away. Of course it was an accident. Ask anyone, I was devoted to that place.

Adding insult to injury, we found out the building had never been owned by the denomination. It technically belonged to Reverend Little's oldest son, who had moved to New York years earlier. When Reverend Little passed, his son planned to keep the building on the land. The fire, however, gave him a chance to sell the land and retire.

The church leaders weren't fazed by it. They found a new property. A new pastor and a new property.

Under this pastor, we would all be going straight to the fire.

"It's a great thing, actually. We will own this building," they said.

Was I supposed to be thrilled by this?

"Well, where's the property?"

"Have you heard of Liberty Bingo Hall?"
Straight to the fire.

CHAPTER 15:
Sprucing Up

Rosling, 2020—I dressed in my oldest jeans and a shirt that I had painted our dining room in as a teenager, and then I threw on an old pair of Converse that had once been white and pulled my curly hair back into a high nest at the top of my head.

"Hey, Lula," I said as I kissed her cheek.

Gentry helped her make tea. He looked at me softly and handed me a cup. I took it but didn't thank him or respond.

"You ready to paint, sweetie?" Lula asked. "You look like you're a professional already. I'd hire ya. Oh, Gentry, I have to tell you about the time she painted the dining room. She wanted to surprise me. I kept telling her that I wanted to paint it a sea-salt color because I love those nautical-blue tones. I must have said it over and over again. Well, one day she took it upon herself—she was twelve, now—to go to the hardware store and buy all the materials with her saved-up allowance money. She was so proud of herself. She taped it all up and painted it. But let me tell you. It looked horrible."

"Is that right?" He laughed.

"It was the sweetest thing anyone had ever done for me, but we spent hours painting over what she painted. We made it work. Like we always did."

"Me and you, Lula. Me and you."

We walked to the car to head to the church. Gentry let Lula in the front seat and then walked around to the driver's side door as I was about to get in.

"Rosling." He opened my door and held out his hand in an attempt to be chivalrous.

"Thanks, but I can get my own door," I said.

"Look, I know this is going to be a challenge for both of us, but I want you to know that I'm trying my best."

"If you are here to disrupt anything or just to prove some kind of point, I will injure your face."

"You'll injure my face?" he asked half serious, half smiling. I couldn't help but grin a bit myself at my inability to intimidate. "Is there any particular method in which you will injure my face?"

"Shut it, Rev," I said, getting into the back of the car.

This was the first of four scheduled church workdays. Four Saturdays in one month was all he was asking for. I assumed there wouldn't be a large turnout, but his youthful presence had struck a chord with many of the younger families who were new to the town.

Our town had really grown since I'd moved away. There were new subdivisions now, and the historic village area that met the water and the covered bridge were bustling with boutiques and kitschy coffee shops now.

Surrounding the village square were more profitable local businesses, historic homes, and railroad tracks that met both creeks and winding hills. The place still kept its charm. The drive through the mountains had little to no cell service but held a kayak-and-bait shop that doubled as a gas station. It became a spot that people passed through for kayaking, ziplining, and whitewater rafting excursions.

On our drive to the church building, I saw the familiar blue '76 Mustang parked outside the hardware store. The same man I had seen with Lula after her doctor appointment was walking out of the store toward the car.

"Lula, do you know that car?" I asked.

Lula looked around, confused, and I immediately felt like an idiot for asking her.

Gentry drove us under the old covered bridge as we neared the new church building, a bingo hall. There was no way to put it gently. The place was ugly.

Mae sat outside with a group of volunteers, ages spanning from late twenties to late seventies. She seemed eager for us to get out of the car, walking directly up to Lula's door and opening it for her.

"If this is the place, if this is really the place, I'm about to have to convert. We can't go from the oldest, finest property in the town to a dilapidated bingo hall. You've got to be kidding me."

"Hi, Mae, and hey, everyone. Thanks for coming out today. This is the first of four workdays. As you can see, it's not much to look at now. But it backs up to the creek, and the surroundings are quite nice. Here are my plans."

He walked through the building, and we followed as he informed us. "We've got a coffee bar here as you walk in on the left, and to the right is a visitors' counter for first-time guests. The bathrooms are past that on the right, and here to the left in this hallway behind the coffee area is where we have three rooms. I figured these would be perfect for the kids' rooms. We just need to figure out where to put their check-in area. But here, right in front of us as you walk through these big double doors after passing this lobby area, is the sanctuary.

"We've got the sound station here in the back. Del, I'm putting you in charge of getting that set up. Make sure you call the electrician about that wire we found. But if you look forward from there, we can fit about one hundred chairs in the sanctuary if you use this seating plan. It still leaves enough room for people to talk and walk around a bit in between services. My favorite part though—my absolute favorite—is right outside these exit doors on either side of the stage here. These lead out to a large deck that overlooks the creek. This is a great place for us to have fellowship, small groups, weddings—you name it!"

We all stared in awe, wondering how this group of maybe twenty people would be pulling this off over the course of four Saturdays. We had to build the stage, set up sound equipment, paint, put in flooring, make the outside not look like a bingo hall, set up kid rooms, and so much more. How? Just how did he expect this to come together?

"I had a guy who was going to help with flooring, but he can't join until next week. Can anyone else take the lead on that this week?"

Someone from the crowd spoke up. "I've torn up and laid flooring before. I can take the lead on that but will need one or two helpers."

"One more thing, guys. These fluorescents have to go. We need some recessed lighting, but really it will be good to open up these windows and bring in as much natural light as possible."

A few younger couples stood awaiting directions from Gentry, who was fidgeting over papers and plans with Mae. Del went to the sound area and got to work.

Gentry looked around at the mess of things that needed to be done and asked one of the women, "How are you with a paint brush?" He made his way over to me next.

"I have to tell you something important," I said.

"What's that?"

"I have no skills. I mean none. Like, even moral support. I'm not even good at encouraging people who are working hard. Should I just go?" I joked, making my best attempt to get out of hard labor.

"You have plenty of skills," Gentry said, shaking his head.

He brought up the right side of his mouth into a smile and said, "Don't worry. We'll find a job for you. If anything, I can have you babysit Mae. I need her to criticize someone else for a bit so that I can focus on getting work done."

"Do you really think we're going to get all this work done in four Saturdays?" I asked.

"Well, no. Of course not. I'll be working throughout the week, and a few people are signed up to help. Your Lula signed you up, by the way."

I shot my best "no" glance his way. "I'm not bluffing. I genuinely have no skills."

CHAPTER 16:

Jest Run

entry, 1998—My knees were pressed up against the back of my new foster dad Riley's seat. He wouldn't scooch up, even a little bit. My new foster sister Jesse had been singing, loudly, since we'd left the gas station, and the more annoyed I was, the more intentional she became.

Jesse was only six years old. She had dark curly hair and was missing her two front teeth. She clenched a stuffed bunny and made it dance around while she sang.

"This is Buns," she said. Her voice was so squeaky she sounded just like a mouse.

"Jesse, I know that's Buns. You've already introduced me to Buns. Remember?"

She twisted her nose at me and looked out the window to show Buns the scenery.

We were on our way to the Blue Ridge Parkway, and we were going to be cutting down our own Christmas tree. The plan was to get hot chocolate and meet with Santa as well on one of the trains that rode through the mountain. At thirteen years old, it was the most magical Christmas I'd been promised in years.

I lifted my legs slightly so that I could give my knees a little bit of breathing room. Catherine, Riley's wife, looked back at me and shook her head. "Stop kicking your dad's seat, or you're not meeting Santa."

"He's not my dad, and I'm not kicking his seat. My knees are folded up. They're cramping."

She shook her head again. "What about you, Jesse? Are you doing okay back there?"

"I'm fine, but Buns is getting hungry," she said.

"Okay, we'll be stopping soon for lunch."

Jesse started singing again and looked directly at me with a giant smile on her face. "We're gonna meet Santa! And you're not getting anything because we all know you aren't good."

I looked over at her and smiled sarcastically. "Santa looks for people who need him the most. I'm always kind, Jesse. So Santa probably likes me better."

You would have thought the car had ran into a pole. Jesse screeched loudly, causing Riley to swerve on the road. He yelled several profanities before realigning the car.

"Santa does not like you better. I heard Riley talking to Catherine, and they both agree that you need a lump of coal for Christmas."

"Oh, Jesse, that's not what we said, honey. Be nice. We said that Gentry has been a little naughty, but everyone still should have a good Christmas."

These fosters were new to the game and trying very hard. I had to applaud them. They really cared and really wanted to enrich our lives. Riley and Catherine had tried hard since day one of me being dropped off. Jesse arrived the same day. She was cute and small and had all the potential of being molded into a great human being still.

I, on the other hand, was a thirteen-year-old boy with a problematic record and a murderous father. They didn't turn either of us away, but it was easy to see that Jesse was the kid they always wanted and I was excess baggage.

"Jesse, can you ask Buns what he wants to eat for lunch?" Catherine asked, laughing.

"Buns wants to eat carrots!" Jesse yelled.

"I'm not sure where we can get Buns carrots right now. Does Buns maybe want a cheeseburger or a hot dog? How about this—if we see a diner anywhere that may have carrots, we will stop there."

Riley was concentrating on the road. Every now and again, he would mutter something undiscernible to Catherine, and she'd reassure him in the same inconspicuous tone, patting his hand while he drove in silence.

Jesse started dozing off, and the bunny fell on the floor. I leaned forward to pick it up and put it back on her lap, but she opened her eyes screaming, accusing me of stealing it.

"I'm not taking it. I was giving it back to you. I swear."

"Listen, guys, that's enough back there until we get to where we are going. Let's just play the quiet game. Gentry, try not to upset your sister."

"She's not my sister," I said.

Catherine looked back at me with a straight face and said, "Well, no. I suppose she doesn't have to be."

I didn't know what to make of what she said, but I knew quickly that she didn't mean to say it out loud. She looked forward again and started crying quietly.

Jesse continued to nag me until we reached a beautiful row of trees with various colors. She was so mystified looking out the window that she decided it was more exciting than trying to get my attention. She was tired of messing with me and was intrigued by the scenery.

I was too engrossed in the surroundings to stay mad. It was a beautiful place.

One week later, the family decided to work through the process of adopting Jesse. They decided that I wasn't a good fit for them.

CHAPTER 17:

Eleanor Chase

Rosling, 2020—"I've got to go see a man about a circuit breaker." I had grown accustomed to hearing Gentry say things like this. Lula said she wanted to tag along, which meant it was best if I'd join as well.

A few people were adding flooring to the nursery area, including Del. The first thing I noticed when I walked into the room was his baby sister. She looked to be about a year old. She was standing in one of the cribs in the room shaking the milky contents of her bottle while Del worked on the other side of the room with two other volunteers.

"Hey there, I see we have a visitor. Who's this?" I never realized how high my voice could get, but something about the baby brought out my inner chipmunk.

Gentry walked toward the baby and picked her up. She didn't seem to mind and leaned her head into his chest while he bounced her around.

"This is my sister Eleanor," said Del.

"Well, hey, Eleanor. It's nice to meet you." Gentry had a chipmunk squeak too. He put Eleanor back in the crib, and she continued to shake the bottle and watch the room in amusement.

Gentry left the nursery to work on his circuit breaker woes while I tried to make myself useful in the nursery somehow.

"Del, do you want me to watch her for a few minutes while you guys work?"

"No, it's okay. She likes being in here with me. She hasn't been fussing or anything." The baby was wearing a pink dress, white shoes, and pink socks. She had her fine hair pulled up into a point on the top of her head. As I was talking to Del, she cooed and entertained herself with making random noises.

"I'll be wrapping up here shortly. This should only take us another hour at the most."

Del continued to surprise me. He loved classic rock and played multiple instruments. He could lay flooring and program a sound system. On top of that, he was okay with babysitting his little sister. I did notice, however, that it was eleven thirty on a Tuesday.

The two men who were helping to put in the flooring walked into the kitchen to eat lunch.

"Del, where do you go to school?"

"I don't go anymore. I dropped out earlier this year."

"Aren't you a senior?"

He wiped some sweat from his head and looked over at me quietly. "You ask a lot of questions." He grinned and wasn't being rude, but I got the message loud and clear. He didn't want to talk about it.

"I'm sorry. Wasn't trying to pry," I said. "Can I help with anything in here?"

"Yes, please, actually. Can you screw the outlet covers back on? Gentry and I painted last week but never came back in to screw them on."

"Oh, yeah, I can definitely handle that." I was excited to have a task that would not be a danger to any inhabitants of the building.

"So my mom's not doing great, and I've been sort of taking care of baby Eleanor. I plan to get my GED. I just couldn't keep going to school because we didn't have anyone to watch her."

I nodded, knowing that he was inviting me in and I shouldn't push for too much information. I wanted to say something but also keep things light. "I'm sorry your mom's sick."

"Oh, I didn't say she was sick. She's not sick. She's just not doing great. In fact, I see her maybe once every two weeks."

"Del, how old are you?"

"I'm eighteen."

"I'm sorry if I'm overstepping my bounds, but that's not okay. You should be in school. Were you supposed to graduate this year?"

"Yeah, I was. I don't want to be rude, but I don't want to talk about it anymore. We're doing fine."

"Okay, please let me know if you ever need anything."

After Del left, I let Gentry know what he had told me. Gentry nodded.

"Are you going to do anything?"

"What would I do? Del's extremely responsible, and he's eighteen. Why would I put them in a situation to be separated and have Eleanor land in foster care?"

"So you're just going to let them stay like that? He dropped out of school."

"Rosling, I understand that this seems very unorthodox to you, but the alternative of that baby being bounced around is definitely not the better option. If I see a need, I'll take action." Gentry spoke calmly but was firm.

"But wouldn't foster care be better for her?" I asked.

"Better than Del? No. Better than the certainty and stability of someone she knows? No. The likelihood of her ending back up with her mom is high. Not to mention in the meantime it is waging psychological warfare on a kid who can't even speak yet."

"I know I'm not the expert, but—"

"Rosling, trust me on this one."

CHAPTER 18:

Anticipation

*R*osling, 1995—Mama had called the night before and said she couldn't wait to come to my party. I woke up at 5:00 a.m. and started cleaning up her old bedroom so that she would feel comfortable and stay. I took Lula's finest tray and set up cups for tea and placed that on a neatly dusted tall dresser. I even dusted off the blinds and wiped down the baseboards. After washing the sheets and a throw blanket, I changed out the light bulb in the lamp so that the room would feel warm and welcoming.

Lula strung up lights in the backyard and covered tables and chairs with various arrangements of fresh flowers. Several of my classmates and their parents arrived. We were playing tag when she walked through the gate. She was wearing jeans and a yellow shirt, and her blond curly hair was cut shoulder length. It complemented her high cheekbones. She was skinny, I remembered thinking. Lula was going to need to fatten her up a little. I would help and make extra bacon on Sunday mornings if that was what she wanted.

I smiled at her, waiting for her to see me, but she must not have recognized me because she walked right past me to Lula and motioned for her to follow into the kitchen.

I followed behind, trying to catch up and get her attention, but neither of them noticed. They started arguing and must not have realized I was standing at the door.

"Look, I came here, didn't I? I'm here now. I can't believe you're already lecturing me." Mama was upset with Lula, but Lula had her "don't cross me" face on.

"Yes, you are here. So please stay. Have you seen her yet? She's really growing into herself."

"Not yet," Mama said. "I'll go back out and look for her."

Mama turned to walk away from Lula and saw me standing in the doorway. Her mouth gaped open, and she looked back at Lula. "Oh my gosh, is that you, Rosling?"

She hadn't seen me since I was a baby. I had seen her in pictures and knew every freckle from studying every portrait I could lay my hands on.

"Yes, that's her. Isn't she something?" said Lula. She smiled at me with pride in her eyes, and warmth stretched across her countenance.

"It's so good to see you," said Mama.

"Are you gonna stay?" I asked her.

Lula and Mama looked at each other, and Mama smiled back at me and said, "Yes, I think I will for a while."

The party went on. Pizza turned to presents, and presents to cake. Mama kept looking around like she was scanning the room for something particular. Didn't seem like she found it.

At one point, I could see a few of the other moms whispering, and I could tell the signs from a mile away. They were looking at her like the other kids looked at me when I got called to the front for the spelling bee. They must have been jealous. Mama looked uncomfortable.

"I've got to run to the car to get your present. I'll be right back." She brushed past me without stopping. I don't know what came over me, but I grabbed at her shirttail.

"Wait," I said as I pulled in for a hug.

She smiled down at me and brushed my hair out of my face before walking to her car. Minutes passed without Mama or any trace of a present. She didn't come back in the house that day or any day after. At that age, I thought it might have been something I had done, or hadn't done.

I cried in Lula's lap for hours that evening, asking her why Mama didn't want me. Lula scratched my back and told me that it wasn't anything I had done.

CHAPTER 19:

Home

entry, 2002—A few days after junior homecoming, Anna Briggs brought me to the apartment of a young couple named Mike and Janice. My right eye was yellow, beginning its journey to turning black. I much preferred to deal with bruises that other people couldn't see. Having to speak to them was essentially insult to injury.

Janice walked to the door first. She was wearing a purple T-shirt, and a white dish towel was hanging over her shoulder.

"I hope you like Italian," she said. "It's the only thing I know how to cook."

"You don't look Italian," I replied.

She had red curly hair that was pulled to the top of her head in a bun. I walked from the small front porch into the living room with my case worker following. It was not a huge place, but I could see two separate hallways on either side, each with two doors; I presumed those were the bedrooms and bathrooms.

In the living room were two blue-and-white-striped sofas atop vinyl hardwood floors. An antique dresser, painted white, was the TV stand, and yellow-and-blue curtains hung on the sliding door that led to a small outdoor balcony.

Mike—I assumed it was Mike—was at the kitchen counter making salad.

"Hey, you must be Gentry," he said. He looked up from what he was doing and kissed Janice on the temple as she walked back in to check on whatever she was cooking. It smelled good.

"Listen," she said, "normally we would have cleaned up a bit. We didn't know we'd be lucky enough to have you over tonight, so we weren't very prepared. It's so nice to meet you."

I looked around again, and the only mess to speak of was the dinner debris on the kitchen counters.

Anna sat next to me on the couch while Mike and Janice told me about my room and bathroom towels. They didn't stop moving but also had an air of being very laid back.

We sat down for dinner, and the case worker nodded my way as she walked out the door. I didn't have a bag. I didn't have anything to change into.

Mike served me a large plate of spaghetti and garlic bread, and the "salad" was a mixture of tomatoes, feta, olives, cucumber, avocado, and croutons. I realized I hadn't eaten since the previous morning. My stomach growled loudly, but I didn't want to be rude and eat fast. So I took deliberate, slow bites and tried not to make too much eye contact. It seemed for a while that they didn't want to talk to me. Every other family I'd been to bombarded me with questions, even down to what had landed me in foster care to start with, as if kids can succinctly verbalize it. Janice and Mike spoke to each other but acknowledged me. They asked me what I liked to do; they didn't ask me whether I liked the food, or how I was in school. As I finished my dinner, I looked up from my plate at both of them.

"I've got you set up in this room over here," said Janice. "There are clothes your size, towels, toiletries, and a few books if you like to read. You can also feel free to turn on the television. I know I sleep better with it on. I've put some eucalyptus oil in your room so that it's a little more cozy. I hope the smell isn't too strong."

Mike laughed and said "hippy" under his breath. She giggled and poked him in the side.

I walked into the bedroom, which was a pale-green color. The full-size bed was made with a blue and white down comforter, and I had a desk, a dresser, and a television. I opened the dresser drawers to find pants, shirts, underwear, and socks—all my size. Two new pairs of tennis shoes were sitting in the closet waiting for me as well.

My bathroom had the same color scheme as my bedroom: pale green and dark blue. It was the first hot shower I'd had in a week. They had stocked it up with shampoo, conditioner, and men's bodywash. I looked in the mirror and didn't recognize myself. My hair had already grown much longer, to the point of strands extending past my ears, but not enough so that it looked like I was growing it out on purpose. And my eyes—my eyes looked terrible.

After the shower I walked out of the room in my brand-new flannel pajamas and stood in silence until Janice and Mike realized I was standing there.

"Oh great, you're probably wanting to rest, I assume?" asked Mike.

I nodded in agreement. I had nothing left in me to speak. There was no way that I could form sentences at this point. I didn't have the energy to be fake. And it was too soon in this new place to get kicked out.

What day was it?

"Tomorrow's Sunday," said Janice. "We were hoping you'd join us for church."

"Sure," I said before walking back into my bedroom to lie down and sleep. What time were these people going to wake me up? And when would I have control over my own life? I hadn't signed up for any of this.

My mom used to take me to church when I was growing up. It was an Episcopal church, and she loved going. We'd sit in the same spot every week, and she'd write a ten-dollar check when the basket was passed. She put on her good perfume and wore her hair down. I remember Daddy always said she looked pretty before we left for church.

I remember she volunteered a lot in the nursery and pulled me along as well. She'd have me hand out crayons to the kindergarten class and sweep up after everyone left.

When Mike woke me up to get ready, he greeted me with a cup of coffee.

"Don't worry; its decaf," he said as he put it down on the table and walked out of the room. "We'll probably leave in about an hour, if that's okay. If you don't want to join, you don't have to."

"No, that's okay. I'll come," I said.

I got up quickly and put on a dark pair of jeans from the drawer and a pair of Nikes. There were a variety of shirts—button-down shirts, collared shirts, and then there was a row of old band shirts. The Ramones? Who were these people?

I selected one of the nicer button-down shirts just in case I needed to dress up. Janice had already made bacon and eggs and offered me a plate. I thanked her and ate quietly again, still taking in my surroundings.

Janice was in a white blouse and had nice boots on, but Mike was in jeans and a collared shirt. They looked like they might just be going out to dinner.

"Am I dressed up enough for this?" I asked.

They smiled at each other, and Janice said, "Yes, but with that black eye, we're going to have a mean game of 'who wore it best' between you and the pastor." I didn't know if I was allowed to laugh, but it was funny. I just stared at her, waiting for her to have a reaction. "I'm sorry," she said. "I never know when my jokes are stupid or great."

Half of my mouth went into an involuntary smile. I thought I might actually like this couple. They were weird and nice.

We arrived at the church, which was a large brown brick building with long hallways of classrooms and a large sanctuary that had stained glass on the windows. I expected hymns and high-heeled shoes, but every person in the building was in jeans. To my surprise, Mike walked up to

KELLY SULLIVAN YONCE

the front of the church and started playing the bass guitar.
I couldn't believe it.

The sermon was about David and Goliath. I remembered hearing the story, but in my current circumstances,
I identified greatly with David. More than anything else,
I realized I hadn't been to church since the last Sunday
that I had gone with my mom. I felt warm and at home,
as if she had wanted me to come back to church for years,
and her baby boy was finally doing it.

As we were leaving the church, Mike and Janice looked
back at me and asked whether I'd consider coming back. I
couldn't verbalize the fact that I didn't want to even leave.

That night felt like the second night in a great hotel.
I wondered how long it would last.

CHAPTER 20:

Book Exchange

entry, 2002—It was impossible to study at Mike and Janice's. It was too quiet and structured. I was used to chaos for background. I went out to prep for a chemistry test and decided the Starbucks in the next county over had a much better smell and far better snacks. Never mind that it took thirty minutes to get there.

I walked in and looked for the best chair real estate. Part of studying in a coffee shop is finding the best seat. I wanted an armchair if possible, so I scoured first for those while I purchased my grande latte. There sat Rosling in a leather armchair, reading.

I grabbed my coffee and approached.

"I can't help but notice there is one free chair. Would you mind if I take it? I promise not to interrupt you while you read."

She looked surprised but softened her face long enough to nod at the chair. I sat down and pulled my chemistry book out to begin studying.

"Do you have Mr. Paxton?" she asked.

"No, Liezel," I said.

"Good luck." She shook her head and continued reading.

"What are you reading?" I asked.

"*Lucky Jim*. It's a satire. I'm reading it for AP English. Do you read?"

I laughed at the question.

"I mean, do you like to read?" She laughed into her book before she looked up at me, waiting on the answer.

"Yes, I try to whenever I'm not studying. But there's not a whole lot of time usually."

"Well, you've got plenty of time to get yourself into trouble."

"I guess you're not wrong there."

"Why do you do it? Your grades are amazing. You're so smart. Why do you throw everything away?"

I didn't answer her because I didn't know how. Just the very act of her telling me I was smart made me want to do something stupid.

"I'm sorry," she said. "It's none of my business."

"No, it really isn't," I answered.

"Well, good luck on your test," she said as she continued reading.

We sat reading and studying in the Starbucks silently for an hour before she got up to head home for her curfew.

"I'd love to read that book when you're finished," I said.

"I'll bring it to you."

The next day when we saw each other at school, she walked to my locker to hand me the book, *Lucky Jim*. I didn't tell her, but I had already read it the previous semester when I took the same AP English course. I just wanted a conversation starter.

I held onto it for a few days and then found my way to her in the parking lot to hand it back. Every few days we would switch books. We'd never discuss the books and never had actual conversations either. This went on for a few weeks.

School was finished, and I hadn't seen her in the cafeteria or parking lot, but I knew she'd probably be at the grill in town because that was where her crowd typically hung out after school. It was a stretch bringing her the book outside school. As I suspected, she was eating with friends. I walked into the grill and sat the book down on her table.

Rosling sat back in the booth while Blake Cunningham stood up.

"What do you want, loser?" said Blake as he pushed me away from the table.

I pushed him back and told him to mind his business.

Rosling stood up and tried to tell him to stop, but he continued pushing me in the direction of the door while the wait staff and manager raised their voices and threatened to call the police. When we approached the door, I turned him around and pulled him out of it and onto the ground.

We spent a minute rolling around and punching each other until we were pulled apart by the restaurant staff.

Our book exchange routine had come to an end.

I'm not sure how she found it, but that night Rosling knocked on the door of my foster home. Mike had just finished doing the dishes, and Janice was elbow deep in a bag of Doritos watching *The Bachelor*.

"Gentry, there appears to be a girl at the door," said Mike.

"Mike, why do you talk like that?" Janice asked. "What do you mean 'appears'? There is or there isn't." She continued watching the rose ceremony before chanting, "Send her home, send her home."

"I'm sorry," I said to Rosling. "She doesn't mean you. Come in."

Rosling laughed before walking into the living room. Janice and Mike stood to introduce themselves, and Mike said that we could sit out on the front porch to talk for a while.

Rosling started the conversation. "I'm really sorry about today. I don't know why he did that. He's not even my boyfriend. Thank you for the book."

"It's really okay. Our friends aren't the same. But don't worry, I'm not blaming you, and I know that's not who you are."

"So are you okay if we keep sharing books then?"

"Rosling, I don't think it's a good idea. I really want stay out of trouble. I really like it here."

"So they're nice to you?"

"All the time."

"I won't be any trouble. We can meet quietly, or if you want, I can introduce you to my friends."

Rosling reached for my hand, and I moved it away quickly. "No."

"Okay, if you don't want to meet them, then..."

We stood up at the same time, but she paused before leaving. I could tell she wanted to say something, but she seemed to be processing her next words. Instead of speaking, she took a step forward and kissed me. As much as I didn't want to stop kissing her, I knew that we lived in two different worlds.

"No, Rosling." I stopped her. "It's not going to work."

With clear defeat in her expression, she walked off the porch and was wiping a tear out of her eyes. I turned to walk into the house.

A few days later, Mike brought in a UPS package and laid it on the counter.

It was from Rosling Landry.

I opened up the package and pulled out the last book. A Bible. There was a note with it.

> Gentry,
> This is my Lula's favorite book. I can't say I've read the whole thing, but it has never disappointed her. Plus, it's confusing enough that you won't get bored.
> Rosling

CHAPTER 21:

The Third Chair

Rosling, 2020—The row of coffee shops and boutiques that lined the water were lit up with twinkle lights. Couples Lula's age were dancing to the live band that was always playing in the square on Friday nights. The downtown area was busier than a standard weekend. The band would likely play for another hour before the sun fully set, and everything in the town would be deep-fried in due time.

Lula and I found a good spot and unfolded our chairs from her wagon before placing a small cooler of Cokes between us. Lula opened up a third chair next to mine and smiled coyly.

"What's the third chair, Lula?"

Gentry lifted his knees and contorted his way through the crowd of families and then sat in the chair next to mine. He was wearing a Captain America shirt and looked like he had gone a day or so without shaving.

"Gentry, I am so excited you're here," said Lula. "I was afraid this was going to be a very boring event. I already feel better."

Lula smirked at me out of the corner of her eye but concentrated on the band as they moved around the stage between sets.

"I hope it's okay that I'm here," he said it to me quietly. "I didn't want to tell your Lula no."

"I do it all the time. It's really not that hard. She usually gets over it."

He nodded and sat back in the chair. They were in cahoots.

"The jawline on that lead guitar player reminds me so much of your grandfather," Lula said. "He took me to a place like this once." I loved hearing stories about her and my grandfather. "It was one of our first dates."

I glanced over at Gentry to find him elbow deep in the cooler, taking out a Dr. Pepper.

"Sorry, I should have asked. Is it okay if I have one of these?"

"Help yourself."

I found myself still being short with him, despite wanting to try harder. Lula was nodding her head to the music.

"They're pretty good," I said.

Parked in front of the old theater was that '76 blue Mustang. I got up to walk toward the car, but the driver jumped in the vehicle and sped off before I had a chance to speak to him.

When I returned, Gentry looked curious.

"I've seen that car a few times since I've been back in town. He's kind of an odd guy. Just stares at me and then rides off."

Gentry lifted his sleeves above his shoulders and flexed a farmer's tan.

"You can put the guns away, Captain America. I don't feel threatened or anything. It's just weird. Wondering if I know him from somewhere, maybe."

We listened to songs a little bit longer while Lula had several conversations on repeat. It was time to walk back to the house.

Gentry offered to drive us home, and we accepted. It was much darker out and starting to get a bit chilly. We invited him in for a little bit, and he sat down on the couch while Lula ran through her routine of getting dressed, taking her meds, and lying down in her room. It was the standard, and she stuck to it well.

She was sound asleep. A lot of my previous Alzheimer's patients needed melatonin to help stay on their sleep routine. Lula was still sleeping well enough that she didn't need it.

Gentry was sitting quietly on the couch looking out the front window to the long driveway.

"I made us some tea," I said.

"Isn't that like sacred around here? Does this mean I'm being initiated?" He took the cup from my hand. "Well, initiated or poisoned, maybe."

I laughed. "No, it's just a peace offering."

I sat down on the couch, leaving one cushion between us. I pulled my favorite blanket onto my lap and faced his direction.

"So Lula is going to die," I said.

"Oh wow, is that what her doctor said?" he asked, seeming far more surprised than I assumed he would.

"No, but that's just what happens. It could be one year. It could be ten. You just never know what kind of progression it's going to be."

I said it so matter-of-factly that it took me a moment to realize I was talking about my own Lula. I had seen it happen over and over to people I was caring for, but never my own Lula.

"How does someone die from it?" he asked.

"It's typically not the Alzheimer's that kills them. It's typically other deterioration and things like pneumonia or falling. Strokes. That sort of thing."

"Based on what you're seeing right now, how long does she have?"

I didn't answer because there was no way for me to ever know. "I have questions for you," I said plainly and sipped my tea.

His hand started shaking around his cup. I could tell he was slightly nervous. "I'm ready," he said.

"If God is real, why do Alzheimer's and cancer exist? Or murder, for that matter? Or terrible people? I've gone my entire life wondering this, and now I just want someone to tell me. Why does the world suck so much if there is a God controlling everything?"

He nodded and took a sip of tea. "Are you interested in me actually answering the questions, or are you venting right now?"

"Both?" I was mainly asking myself. "Yes, both."

"Okay, want to start with murder or Alzheimer's?" he asked.

"Oh, I didn't know the answer would get that intricate. Let's go murder first."

He shook his head and put down the cup so that he could speak with his hands. I hadn't realized it would turn into a sermon.

"So, for murder, I have something of an analogy. Let's say every single day growing up, your Lula told you that the number-one rule was to tell her that you loved her. Let's say that was her rule. Would she ever know that you really mean it?"

"I mean, to some degree, yes, but I think I see what you're saying."

"Well, God wants us to love Him, and He wants us to choose good over evil, but He doesn't force us to make good decisions. And whether we like it or not, sin exists. He didn't create it. We made that decision and fell from grace, but He's also not a puppeteer forcing us to be good people or to choose to have a relationship with Him. That's where our ability to reason comes into play. I can make choices, and one of those choices is whether I want to be good or bad. He's not sitting up in the sky dangling us in front of danger.

"It's also important to say that we shouldn't just go around sinning because He will forgive us. A decision to have a relationship with Him should simultaneously be a decision to try our absolute best not to sin. We shouldn't be abusing His grace. Does that make sense?"

"I'm with you so far," I said.

"Sometimes people aren't going to choose to be good. My dad chose to kill someone. The world is imperfect. There has always been suffering, and there will always be suffering. We weren't promised that everything would be easy. We were promised that if we choose Him, it will all be worth it. One day there will be no more tears or mourning or pain."

"What about Alzheimer's? Or cancer?" I asked.

"God's not sitting up in the sky handing out diagnoses. The world is full of terrible things, and life is really difficult sometimes. But when we choose God, we are choosing to be faithful when things are bad and when things are good. Lula knows God didn't give her Alzheimer's."

"I get that," I said. "What I don't get is that He allows it to happen."

"Do you know what Lula said when she got her Alzheimer's diagnosis? Do you know what she prayed?"

"No, but I'd like to."

"She prayed for your courage and strength. She didn't pray for God to take it away. She prayed that God would give you peace. She didn't pray that God would help her out of it. But she prayed that God would get you to the other side of it."

"Fine. She hasn't prayed for it to be taken away. But it still doesn't explain why He let her get it in the first place, Gentry," I said.

"I don't have all answers, but I can tell you that if I turn off this light and you can't see me, I'm still in the room. What's true in the light when everything is good is also very much real in the dark. We have to look for Him in the harder situations. But He's there. I promise."

"Okay, let's change the subject," I said.

Gentry picked his drink up and pulled one of the pink fluffy pillows behind his lower back. I smiled at this.

"I don't want to change the subject yet," he said.

"Will the church building be ready before Lula's eightieth birthday? I'm hoping to have her party there."

He rolled his eyes at me. "Yeah, it should be. I hope so, anyway."

"It's okay if we use it for her party, right?"

"Yes, it's definitely okay," he said. But I could tell he was getting annoyed. "Can we switch back for a minute?"

"To the other conversation? No," I said.

"But I don't know if I answered your question."

"Let's call a rain check on that discussion," I suggested.

Gentry left for the evening, and I was more confused and frustrated than before. The answer was nice, but I still felt empty. I knew one thing about Gentry, though. He had the same goodness that Lula had.

The plan was to meet up with Gentry at the church building the following morning. I brushed my teeth and changed into my pajamas before checking on Lula and heading to bed to read for a few hours.

CHAPTER 22:

Not All Who Wander Are Lost

osling, 2020—Lula's wrought iron bed was made up with tan-and-pale-pink sheets. The room was pristine.

I looked around the bedroom before making my way into her prayer closet and the bathroom. She wasn't there. I ran around the house yelling her name from room to room with no reply. She was AWOL.

My cell phone had no charge, so I went to the house phone and dialed Gentry. It rang for about twenty seconds without answer, so I slammed it down and ran out the front door to begin looking. I yelled her name into the trees as I ran around the side and backyard. The cars were still there, and I didn't see any footprints or evidence that she had walked off anywhere.

I hadn't changed out of my pajamas yet and didn't have shoes on. I was taking giant breaths of the morning air trying not to panic.

I ran back in the house to dial 911. As soon as the operator answered, I saw Gentry pulling up the driveway.

I ran back outside to tell him what was going on and saw Lula sitting in the passenger side.

Had he found her?

They both got out of the car, laughing and talking like there was no concern.

"You found her. I was so worried." I hugged her tight.

"Found me?" She tilted her head to the side. "Honey, we didn't want to wake you. Gentry took me to breakfast this morning."

Something inside of me snapped, and I stormed back into the house in tears. They yelled after me, but I got right into the shower and didn't wait for either to explain.

CHAPTER 23:

David Lee

*K*atie Lee, 1995—There was no one in town like David Lee.

"Black Velvet" was playing while he approached. I felt like the song could have been written about him.

The room was full of people, but he set his sights on me. His smiled looked well cared for. One of the first things I thought about him was that he likely had good insurance and a dental plan. I wasn't wrong.

My girlfriends dragged me out that night to a crowded party for New Year's Eve. The restaurant was full of party-goers ready to make resolutions and become new people after a night of the same old traditions.

I knew better than to walk out the door with him, but I was bored and he was interesting. He drove slow, but we moved relatively quickly, and the rest was history.

"Katie," he started, "will you marry me?"

"David Lee, are you asking me to run away with you?"

"No, I'm asking you to plant roots with me."

I felt special in his truck, his right hand on my knee. He came from far better circumstances than I did, and we both knew it. He didn't make a habit of reminding me of it, so I liked him even better.

We parked the car in random empty lots so that we could talk longer before he dropped me off. Talking. That wasn't at all what he wanted, but I can't say that I minded at the time.

After two months, I learned I was pregnant. I thought I might as well have been in heaven. I never wanted for a thing while I was pregnant with Gentry. David was kind and had to be the best thing that ever happened to anyone. Until he wasn't.

For nine months it was just him and me. At the end of my pregnancy, a few days before my actual due date, I developed preeclampsia. My kidneys were on overdrive, and my blood pressure was too high, so they wheeled me back for a C-section. I remember being sweaty and light headed. My vision was blurred, and my fingers felt like Twinkies.

They sat me up straight on the table while they did a spinal injection to numb the lower half of my body. Then they quickly positioned me lying down and pulled up a curtain so that I couldn't see what was happening. I felt them moving around my abdomen, working, but I didn't feel pain or know precisely what they were doing.

When they held Gentry above the curtain, it was a new kind of love, something I'd never experienced. I don't think anyone ever loved me that way, and I don't think I'd ever love anyone else the way I loved him.

Gentry and I stayed in the hospital for two weeks with not one visitor. David dropped in every other day to kiss me on my forehead, and then he went home to tend to the house. He said he was going to make up the bedroom really nice for both of us so that Gentry would feel at home right away.

When it was time for us to go home, some switch inside David just flipped. He just stayed aloof. The more Gentry cried, the worse it became.

After about a week of being home, Gentry was asleep on my chest, and I was still having some trouble getting around easily. I asked for a glass of lemonade. David told me that I needed to stop being so dependent on him and get up and fix it myself.

In my hormones I cried and called him a jerk. He'd barely held the baby at all.

Fast-forward through years of ups and downs. Aloof turned to angry. Angry turned to mean. Mean turned to abusive.

Eventually, when Gentry was ten, I met Bill. Bill was never mean.

When David left for work, I started drinking and packing. Bill's wife saw us eating lunch, and it was only a matter of time before David found out. I didn't want him to kill me, so I decided it was best to leave before he returned.

Bill had already decided to stay with his wife, Mae. He told me as soon as she found us. He said it was a mistake. It was a mistake for me, too, but I still knew that it was time to leave David.

Packing to leave Gentry was the hardest thing I've ever done. It left me with an emptiness that I can't describe. I

had no way of feeding the boy, and had no place to go. He had to stay with his dad, and I'd send for him later.

The sadness overtook me, and I continued to fill the glass as the tears fell.

I finally realized there'd be no way I could leave without Gentry. But how on earth could I stay? I'd write the letter, because David needed to know. If he didn't kill me, one day I'd be strong enough and smart enough to get out. When I did, I'd have my boy with me.

I started to feel ill, like I needed to rest quickly. I wrote the letter to David and intended to make my long-term plans when I woke up. I'd start by throwing out the scotch.

> David,
> If you haven't figured it out yet, I've been unfaithful to you. But if you're honest with yourself, you've been unfaithful to me too—every time you've broken the vows to love, honor, and cherish me. You do none of these things. I plan to leave you. The same way you mentally left me a long time ago.
> Katie

CHAPTER 24:

Grace and Identity

Rosling, 2020—Gentry and Del set up stringed lights to span from one side of the sanctuary to the other. The overhead recessed lights weren't working yet, and this would be the first official service in the new building. Chairs were lined up in slightly disheveled rows. The floors and paint throughout were almost ready, and one of the restrooms was functioning. I looked around at how much we had been able to get done in the two weeks we had been renovating so far. Gentry stood under the twinkle lights greeting the church members from the old building and smiling at new faces from the community who had never stepped foot into the previous sanctuary.

Gentry was dressed in a striped button-down shirt with his jeans and Nikes. Lula walked onto the stage and sat behind the keyboard. Del was in his place already, and as the crowd settled and sat for worship, Gentry made his way over to the stage. A teenage girl I hadn't met yet welcomed everyone to the new building.

"We are all first-time guests tonight," she said, "but we are first-time guests in a church home that Jesus has blessed us with. This is our space to worship together. This is our space to introduce the community to Jesus. This is our space to come together as a family of believers."

The music started with mostly acoustic and keys. Gentry played with his eyes closed, and his head tilted back facing the ceiling. The girl sang a song about us all being broken and God using that brokenness to make something beautiful. The keys were beautiful. Lula didn't miss a beat.

After a few songs, the band rested their instruments on the stage and took seats in the front row. Gentry put on a headset microphone and moved to center stage. I'll admit I was very interested in hearing him preach.

"We are all here in this building for different reasons. Some of us felt a conviction or a call from a young age, and nothing can keep us away from a church service. Some of you were invited, and you're just trying to figure out what all this Jesus stuff is. Some of us—some of you like me—have spent your entire lives running as far away from Jesus as possible only to find that He was literally right beside you the entire time. Whichever one of these stages you are in today, your perception of who you are to Jesus is greatly molded by your own perception of who you are. I have news for you. You are all big messes that matter greatly to God." He opened up his Bible, placed it on the black podium in front of him, and then took a sip of his water.

"Open up your Bibles with me, or if you don't have them, don't worry—I don't talk too fast. You can also pull up your Bible on your phone. But again, I'll try not to leave anyone in the dust." He smiled and looked around the room. There were faces of young and old and of various races and ethnicities.

"Today we are going to start a new series titled Grace and Identity. I'm sort of giving away the punch line here, but one thing we need to understand is that our understanding of grace is very much tied to our understanding of identity. For the next four weeks, we will discuss these two principles, but I want us to do a few things differently. I'm only going to preach for about twenty-five minutes, and then we are going to break out in group discussions." The crowd looked around, some of them smiling and some of them appearing uncomfortable with the idea.

"Starting out in the book of John, chapter 4, we are going to look at the story of Jesus and the Samaritan woman." He read John 4, verses one through thirty, and then began speaking again.

"You see, Jesus traveled into this village, and He's talking to this woman—real talk here—about her identity and the labels that have been placed on her by both herself and her village. She's telling Jesus that her background as a Samaritan plays a role in how He should approach her. And He reminds her of some truths about her life that have molded the way she thinks about herself and the way others think about her. How often, church, do we decide to steer clear of Jesus because we assume that He wouldn't associate with someone like us? How often do we miss the opportunity to share our testimony in a way that may actually bring other people closer to Christ? Are we walking around in judgment of ourselves and others, or are we walking around trying to understand who we really are in Christ?"

A few heads in the room were nodding as he continued. He walked around the stage and made eye contact with a few people before his eyes landed on mine. He and Lula were cut from the same good cloth, with the high thread count.

"We have to align ourselves to a few important truths. Write these down, or if you don't have anything to write with, go ahead and text it to yourself so you can look at it and remember this week. We will go more thoroughly into these truths in our breakout discussions. Here they are: we need to understand who Jesus is, we need to understand who we are to Jesus, and we need to understand that our true identity is built upon those two foundational blocks."

We broke out into groups as the band played softly in the background. I sat with a small group under the twinkle lights to the sounds of acoustic guitar, hearing the people next to me explain parts of their lives that they'd never shared with anyone. Hugs were exchanged; real-time therapy was given between perfect strangers. Community was built in a thirty-minute sitting. I listened without sharing.

Gentry went back to the middle of the stage to pray and release the congregation.

"Next week we are continuing our series on identity and grace. For the next three weeks, we will discuss testimony, then judgment, and finally forgiveness. I've got some great videos to show you as well. I hope I see you all during the week in passing. We've still got a lot to do around here, and many hands make light work. Go in the grace of Christ this week."

Some people left right away, while others stayed behind talking. Del, always busy, started packing up instruments before picking up his baby sister from the nursery. Lula and Mae walked over to Gentry and me. Lula shared her feelings first.

"It's been a long time since we've heard a message like that, Reverend." She smiled and nodded, giving her approval.

Mae stood quietly and looked in the direction of the door.

"Great job tonight. And great crowd," said Lula. "How'd you get these people to come?"

"I invited them."

Lula chuckled and grabbed Mae's arm. "Mae, he invited them. Why didn't we think of that?" she said, laughing.

I nodded at Gentry and started slow clapping as the rest of the room cleared out.

"Yeah, yeah, yeah," Gentry said. "I know. You don't think much of me or Jesus. I'm glad you came for Lula, though." He smiled and grabbed his Bible from the podium. "I'll walk y'all out, if you don't mind."

I didn't mind. "No, really. I think it was great. I still don't buy any of it. But that being said, I'll see you next week."

I opened my car door, and Gentry opened his.

"Actually, I'll see you tomorrow. You have more piano lessons, and there's lots of work to do here. Don't disappoint Lula, now." He waved his finger at me and got into the car.

CHAPTER 25:

Let's Make a Deal

Rosling, 2020—Gentry still had the same freckles he had as a kid. His face was much more grown up now, but those freckles continued to bring his edge down. I was used to picking at him and said, "You should let your beard grow out. Not a homeless-style beard but like a nice edging around your face. It might enhance those freckles you've got."

"I can't pull off a beard," he said.

"You definitely can. You're rocking some lumberjack style anyway. It's like a cross between mountain man and hipster. A beard would suit you."

He rubbed his chin and shook his head from side to side. "My face is so handsome. Why would I ruin a good thing?"

"Okay, back to the lesson." He was joking, but I definitely found myself holding my breath when he sat next to me.

"Right. This is middle C."

"I'm aware that this is middle C. I have the chords down now. Just not some of the minors and majors."

"Do you want help or not?"

"Is that a serious question? I didn't ask for help, Gentry. You're giving an unsolicited piano lesson."

"Right. That's right. Well, shut up anyway, because I can't hear myself being smart. The majors and the minor chords really are not too complicated but can seem hard at first if you overthink it. Try jumping from each specific minor to the next. Like from A minor to B minor then to C minor. Kind of like when you were learning just the chords. You can really do this until your hands naturally jump where they are supposed to. And then you can switch to majors and do the same. In the meantime, you can keep learning songs that have one or two majors or minors in them until you master that. Then we will learn the other chords. That's where things get a little more complicated."

"Okay, slow down for a second. Don't think too far ahead. Minors today and tomorrow right?"

"Yes, minors and majors today and tomorrow. Some of the regular chords that you learned are actually the majors. Like when you learned D—that's already D major."

I stared at him blankly.

"I'm not trying to confuse you, I swear. Okay, I'll leave you to it. Do you guys have any stuff to make sandwiches?"

He disappeared into the kitchen while I kept practicing. I was able at this point to very simply play the four songs they had taught me. I did it well enough that I wasn't messing up, but I couldn't play without looking away from the keys. So when it was time to turn the sheet or look at a different section, I had to figure out again where to place my hands, and the song would leave me in the dust.

"It's sounding good, Rosling!" he yelled from the kitchen with a mouth full of Muenster cheese. "You don't suck so much today."

Lula emerged from her bedroom in her nightgown and walked through to kiss my temple. She turned to find Gentry and immediately yelled at him to get out of her kitchen.

"I need to go into town today to get more tea and other groceries," said Lula.

"I can take you in a little bit," I replied. "Listen to this, Lula."

I played her one of the songs that I was doing well at so far, and she nodded in approval.

"That's great, honey. Regular Beethoven."

"No kidding, right?"

"I'm gonna go get dressed for the day, and then I need to go into town for coffee and other groceries."

"Okay, Lula."

Lula walked into her room, shutting the door behind her, and Gentry reemerged to join me on the piano bench. He smelled like cheese.

"When your hands jump, your pinky is going rogue. You've got to get that beast under control, Rosling."

He demonstrated, and I tried it myself, my pinky still sticking straight into the air instead of hitting the proper key.

"Work on that because the note is not going to sound full if you aren't hitting it."

Lula came back out of her room still in her nightgown. "Good morning, you two." She walked around confused for a second.

"Lula, are you going to get dressed so that we can go get some tea?"

"You can have tea here, Rosling. I don't know what it is with having to get tea out. Is it just the experience of it?"

"No, I mean we are going to go to the store to pick more up so that we can have tea here."

"Oh, okay, you want to go out? That's good. Do I stay here?"

"No. Why don't you go get dressed, and you can come with?"

"Okay." She walked through the hall and passed her bedroom. "What do I do?" she asked.

"You can just go into the room and pick out some clothes, and then we can get going."

She stood still for a minute staring at me, and it registered that she didn't know what to do. She didn't know how to go into her closet and pick out an outfit and clean herself up to get ready to go.

"It's okay. I'll come with you. I'll help, Lula." I looked over at Gentry and couldn't stand the pout on his face, so I joked, "Gentry, keep practicing. You sound terrible."

I laid out the clothes for Lula, and she held each item up, looking at it intently. I wasn't ready for this stage yet, but I was sure she wouldn't be either if she knew what was going on.

I helped her figure out how to get dressed and brush her teeth, and I could tell she was getting more agitated by the minute. Frustration and disappointment are two of the most painful parts of Alzheimer's. She knew that she wasn't figuring it out, and she knew that something was missing in her mind.

We went out to pick up the tea, and Gentry helped us bring in the other groceries. Lula walked around a bit confused before sitting in front of the piano and playing songs that she had always played while I was growing up.

Gentry and I wandered to the front porch and drank our tea together, and he looked at me like he wanted me to speak.

"What? Why the death stare?"

"Have you found a way to reach out to your mother?"

I laughed at him and shook my head. "Why?"

"Because she needs to know. That's her mom. She needs to be here."

"Yeah, she also needed to be here for me when I was a child, but that didn't happen. Why would I reach out? She's not going to come back for us. For her."

"You never know what she'll do until you try. Is there a number you can try? A contact?"

"Lula has always kept tabs on where she's living. I know she has the information. But why do I need to use it? How is it my responsibility to call her for anything at all?"

I knew he was right, but I wanted to be willful about this as long as possible.

"Your old issues with your mom or even your current issues with your mom don't distract from the fact that if her mother has an incurable disease, you need to make her aware. It's not your job to make her do the right thing. It's your job to do the right thing and tell her."

Why did he have to be right?

"The right thing? You want me to reconcile because you're so peaceful these days. She doesn't deserve to be here. She doesn't deserve to help her in this stage of her life. And besides, you need to concentrate on yourself, and don't try to save me anymore. I've got it covered, and your advice isn't welcome at all."

"Okay, yeah, I need to do some healing of my own. I'm back here, right? At least I'm trying."

"Oh, you're trying? Just because you are being nice to someone that you were awful to your entire childhood doesn't mean you are trying. Have *you* reached out to your dad? Have *you* tried to connect with him? Until you can bring yourself to do that, leave me out of your crusades."

He shook his head and looked up to the sky with his eyes closed long enough for me to wonder if he was praying or exaggerating his annoyance with me.

"Okay, I'll make a deal with you. I'll go see my dad in prison if you call your mom."

"You spend a lot of time meddling in my household, Gentry."

"That's fair. But is it a deal?"

"Fine. But you're going first."

"Only if you come with me."

CHAPTER 26:

Prison

Rosling, 2020—I waited on the porch and watched Gentry pull in to the long gravel driveway. The four-hour drive would likely be awkward, so I packed a book into my oversized tote. When he got out of the car, he ran past me into the house.

"I'm gonna say hi to Lula and Del first," he said. Del and his baby sister were sitting with Lula that day so that Gentry and I could take the trip.

"When are the visiting hours?" I asked. I wasn't trying to rush him, but something was telling me he was trying to procrastinate.

He was already up the steps, letting himself into the house and walking directly to the kitchen. Lula had been up since 6:00 a.m. She used to have breakfast going by the time I'd roll out of bed. Three days ago we stood at the microwave, and I told her which button would heat up her leftovers. She was frustrated.

I didn't follow Gentry into the house. He eventually walked back outside and asked whether I packed enough snacks for both of us.

"I forgot to pack snacks," I said as I ruffled through my bag.

"Oh," he said, "we'd better fix that."

After he pulled into the gas station, he tapped my knee and said, "Stay here." I hesitated, but he said he had an important surprise. He emerged from the store with two glass Coke bottles and a bag of boiled peanuts.

"This is how you road trip."

"Take a lot of road trips growing up, did you?" I regretted my stupid question immediately.

"My dad used to take me all over to go fishing. I made a few other random trips too."

I remember taking many trips over the summers with Lula through the Smoky Mountains and to waterparks, museums, and beaches a few hours east.

He held the soda out toward me with mischief in his grin. "You can't ride without this."

"Okay, you have my attention," I said, grabbing the cold soda.

Southern backroads through the mountains become a resounding mark on a kid's memory. Produce stands and cabins that sell kayaks become landmarks that sketch nostalgia into you. Vines hug their way up trees that just about touch the sky, and as the landscape changes, you don't know whether you're in the mountains or near the ocean. Depending on where you are in North Carolina, it could be either. Bits of the sun shine through the trees, creating a kaleidoscope effect on the black roads as the wind blows branches to and fro.

"You want the windows down?" he asked, his eyes lingering in my direction a few seconds longer than they should. I stared back, and my right hand naturally moved to the door to roll it down. I didn't answer him directly.

"So where do we go when we get there?" I asked.

In part I was trying to make conversation to break the silence, but I also always have to have a plan. Even if the plan doesn't impact me, I still have an undeniable obsession with orchestrating all the situations around me.

He stared ahead and put his left elbow on the door to help prop up his head while his right hand continued driving. I fought the urge to tell him to use ten and two.

"I'm not sure really. I'll try to check with whoever is at the front and ask what I need to do to see him. Then I'll wait."

"When's the last time you saw him?" I asked.

He didn't look back in my direction and didn't answer for a few minutes. "That day in court."

He had been ten years old, and now it was twenty-five years later. It hit me even harder knowing that this was the first time his dad would see him as an adult. He had grown up four hours from his dad, and no one had ever brought him to visit.

"Do you want me to stop asking you questions?" I asked.

He smirked and looked at me, smiling with his teeth now. "That was also a question."

I laughed, but it cracked through my nervous shell, and I wiped a bead of sweat off my temple knowing that I had no idea how to be alone with him. We had spent the greater part of our lives blaming each other for everything bad that ever happened. Now we were taking care of a person together, building a church together, and so on. We were learning to heal from our pasts—together.

"I'd like to ask you a question, Rosling," said Gentry.

"Okay, I'm ready."

"Why aren't you married?"

I exaggerated a laugh. "I've had a few relationships over the years, but they've been very surface level. I put a lot of myself into my work and don't regret that at all. What about you?"

"Well, I've barely dated over the past few years. I put a lot of myself into my work as well, I guess."

"Let's put some music on," I suggested, and took a drink of my Coke.

He turned on the radio and scanned through the stations until he finally gave up.

"What's the problem?" I asked.

"None of this is road trip music," he said.

He fiddled with his phone for a moment and then smiled as he pressed the Bluetooth button.

"This will do. Let me ask you. Ever sing 'Row, Row, Row Your Boat'?"

"Yes?" I answered with a lot of confusion.

"Well, this is the southern version of that."

Doobie Brothers' "Black Water" started playing, and he immediately began dancing.

"Okay, now," he said. "You've got to sing the good parts at the right time; otherwise, you'll ruin it."

I had no idea what he was talking about.

"Well, I built me a raft, and she's ready for floatin'. Oh Mississippi, she's calling my name."

I was laughing and trying my best to sing the parts I knew.

"Okay, this part's important." He grabbed my hand and waved it in the air.

"Okay, I'm ready."

I sang as loud as I could. That was when it all fell apart. I sang everything all wrong from there, but he sang both parts so loud it didn't even matter.

"Old Black Water, keep on rolling," Gentry sang and then pointed at me to finish.

"Mississippi moon, won't you keep on shining on me?"

"Okay, you're kinda good, but you're also kinda lousy," he yelled over the music. "You have to get into it, or you're ruining everything."

We were both laughing now.

"Ruin everything? That's a lot of pressure."

He started the song over several times while I continued to do a mediocre job.

We moved on to Marshall Tucker Band and Creedence Clearwater Revival.

He sang everything, and I found myself singing along too. I didn't touch my book once.

We arrived at the state prison shortly after 1:00 p.m. We sat in the parking lot for over twenty minutes while he stared at the building. He seemed composed, not shaking or breathing heavily. No bead of sweat to give away whatever was going on inside his head.

"Are you sure you want to come with me?" He broke the silence but still stared forward at the concrete sidewalk leading its way up to what looked like a very heavy door. "You don't have to do this. Why are you doing this for me? I was horrible to you."

"Grace," I said, putting my left hand on top of his right and squeezing tightly. "Good ole-fashioned grace."

His eyes softened, and he shook his head before looking out the window again. "Ah, so you learned something at church then," he said.

"And because I really love a spectacle."

His laugh came from his belly now, and he looked at me with small tears building in the corners of his eyes. "Okay, let's go."

We both got out of the car and met on the concrete walkway. He pulled the giant metal door and was greeted by several armed guards and a man at a front door. Literal gatekeepers.

Gentry said hello and started filling out paperwork to check in.

"Is she coming in too?" asked the guard.

"It's up to you," he said.

"Yes, of course. I want to be with you," I said, and he smiled. "I mean help you. I want to be there for you." He was laughing again.

I had to fill out paperwork and provide my ID. We were brought down a long hallway, where they searched us both before letting us into a common area with long wooden tables. And then we waited.

I sat next to him on one side of the table. He grabbed my hand and started praying out loud for his composure and forgiveness, things I had long ago decided weren't necessary to be a good person. Gentry was starting to convince me that these were the only things that we actually need in our toolkit to be remarkable.

The clank of a large door drew our attention to a guard escorting Gentry's dad into the room.

He was wearing a beige prison jumpsuit but wasn't in cuffs. He had a close shave that made his jawline very prominent. He was still a dapper-looking southern man, as though hard time hadn't taken away the genteel. Moreover, I could see so much of Gentry in his countenance. He walked to the table with the guard behind him, and the fish tattoo peeked out of the sleeve of his shirt.

He sat down without speaking. His face was soft, but he seemed surprised to see Gentry. It felt like an hour passed before either of them spoke. They continued shifting glances, but both of them looked down for a while.

Gentry's dad, David, spoke first.

"I'm sure it took a lot for you to get here. I'm sure it wasn't an easy road for you. I'm sorry that I missed so much. I'm sorry that I was angry."

I started crying randomly, and both of them looked at me. I knew it would not be easy to see Mama after all this time and wondered how Gentry was keeping his composure.

"Is this your wife?"

"No, an old friend. A new friend."

"Forgive me," I said. "I don't know how to act in social situations." They both looked at me as though I had lost my mind.

"I would have brought you something," Gentry said. "I didn't know what you may need."

"I'm good here. I'm just surprised to see you. And happy."

Gentry sat in silence. I broke the silence when I accidentally stubbed my toe kicking the leg of the table.

"Would it be okay if I continue to visit you?" Gentry asked him.

His dad smiled at the question. "That'd be great. Tell me about your life. Are you married? Where do you live?"

"Who raised me?" he cut in.

I didn't expect the question. Neither did his dad.

"Who raised you?" he asked with his hands resting on the table and his palms up. "You may think I don't want to know. But I'm ready to know the hard stuff. I want to know everything. We can't get to the good if I don't deal with the bad."

"I was raised in eight different foster homes." He wiped a few tears from his eyes.

"Did you graduate high school?"

"Yes, at the top of my class. I was a great student, like you always told me. I just had anger issues at home. So my foster parents typically had a hard time. One couple introduced me to church. They introduced me to Jesus."

"So you're a Christian?"

"I'm a pastor."

His dad sat back in his chair and nodded. The weight of the statement clearly took his breath away. He moved his hands to his lap and wiped his palms across the legs of his beige pants.

"So you preach forgiveness."

"I believe in forgiveness. I am thankful for forgiveness. I have faith in forgiveness. But I can't say I always understand it."

At that statement, his dad nodded again and looked toward the guard, whose attention was on another inmate getting too close to his visitor.

"I guess that makes sense. But do you practice the same forgiveness you preach about?"

I couldn't look away now if I wanted to. The wide-eyed stare down that was happening was a combination of passive-aggressive father-son debate and the most existential conversation I've ever been privy to.

"I do practice it. I work at it every day. I'm getting better at it every day." Gentry said.

His dad let out an exhale that must have been stuck somewhere deep down in his bowels because he appeared to be breathing normally until that moment, but I guess he hadn't been breathing at all.

"I am sorry. There's not a single day that I don't wake up and remember how I hurt you. That I took a man's life. That I broke your mother's heart. That the pieces of my life that fell apart will never actually be put back together. I remember every single day that no matter what happens when I get out of here, I'm not going to the home I knew.

I've hurt the most important people in the world. I've hurt you. I know this daily, son. I'm sorry."

It was against the rules, but Gentry stood to hug his dad over the table. The guard started hollering at them and walked over and hit the table gently with the stick. "You've got to sit down, David. You can't be doing that."

"I'm sorry," he said, and sat back down, wiping his eyes with his sleeves.

They sat, they talked, they forgave. Why was it so easy for him to forgive his father? He had lost his mother. He had grown up in foster care.

I sat quietly while they finished their talk.

"So what do you do around here for fun?" Gentry asked, attempting to lighten things up a little.

"I run the Sunday church service and weekly Bible studies," answered David.

Gentry smiled and nodded.

"Of course you do," I said it sarcastically, and out loud on accident.

They looked at me and continued talking for a few more minutes.

"All right David, wrap it up," said the guard.

"It was so good to see you. Thank you for coming," said David.

Gentry promised he'd visit once a month until his release, which would be in just a few more years.

I couldn't turn off the anger. What gave this man who had destroyed my childhood the ability to be such a great human now? Where were his morals then? Not to mention what he had done to his son. Then there was the situation with my mama. She abandoned me, and the only person who ever cared about me was going to die. But before she'd die, she'd forget me, and I'd have to watch the better part of her wither away completely. It's a terrible thing to watch the erosion of a person's mind. When it's someone like Lula, it's inconceivable.

My expectations and anger got the better of me, and I clenched my hands in my jean pockets as we walked out of the building. They searched us again and signed us out. We walked silently back to the car. I wanted to throw a fit, but it wasn't my fit to throw. This wasn't my time. Gentry had just done the impossible, and I wanted to break a window because I couldn't do the same.

He seemed calm as he backed out of the parking space. We drove along in silence for the first hour, nothing on the radio. By my calculation we'd be home as the sun was setting. I looked out the window at the pretty wildflowers that covered the highway mediums.

Gentry turned on another song, but in lieu of classic rock, he introduced me to something new.

"This is Bryan and Katie Torwalt," he said. I listened intently because the voices were so steady and immediately drew me in. It wasn't cheesy. I didn't feel like I was in a chapel. It created a lump in my throat.

"When you walk into the room, sickness starts to vanish, every hopeless situation ceases to exist, and when you walk into the room, the dead begin to rise 'cause there is resurrection life in all you do."

I began sobbing uncontrollably in the passenger seat. Gentry pulled off the road until I composed myself. I jumped out of the car on the side of the highway, daylight starting to fade. He pulled me in for a hug and rested his chin on the top of my head.

"I don't understand," I sobbed. "I don't understand how you were able to forgive him so easily."

"I'm sorry for what I asked you to do that day, Rosling," he said. "I'm sorry I asked you to lie. And I'm sorry for everything else after that."

I knew it wasn't his fault. I was relating to him in a way that I hadn't expected. He was just a kid. He was scared, and he grew up without a real family. This was something I'd have to learn to not hold against him. I just didn't know if I'd ever understand how he was able to show so much grace in this situation.

When we reached town, it was dark out. He pulled up the long drive to Lula's and got out to open my door. He walked me up to the porch. I was thankful I had remembered to leave the lights on before leaving that morning. As I walked in, he grabbed my hand to pull me back around and kissed me. It was our first kiss since we had parted ways in high school.

After embracing it for a second, I jumped back and asked, "Are you allowed to do that?"

He laughed and said, "Well, I probably should have asked first, but yes."

I realized I was still holding on to his wrist and abruptly let go. He looked at my hand and laughed.

"All right, it's your turn. Call your mom. Tonight."

"No."

"What do you mean, no?" he said. "We had a deal."

"Okay, fine."

I walked in and slammed the screen behind me. Del was sitting on the couch rocking his sister, and Lula had already gone to bed. I saw them out and decided that I'd wait a few more days to place my call to Mama.

CHAPTER 27:

Testimony

Rosling, 2020—Gentry welcomed everyone walking into the church building, shaking hands and asking people about their plans for the coming week. He sipped on a cup of coffee while he spoke. I could see his eyes following me sporadically as I moved about the room. I grinned each time I caught him, and he'd refocus on the conversation at hand.

The band played well that day, and I was looking forward to next week's service, where I'd play for the first time in front of the congregation.

After the band gently put down instruments and left the stage, Gentry moved to the front and positioned his headset mic to begin his sermon.

"Last week we started the series on grace and identity. I hope you've all had a chance to be in the Word this week and have challenged yourself by practicing some of what we discussed. Today is an important part of this series, but it's also the hardest for me. We are talking about testimony.

"I know that many of you have an idea about who I am and where I came from. Some of you more than others, maybe. Most of you know that I grew up in the foster system. Most of you probably know that my father has been in prison since I was ten and that I lost my mom the same day that I lost my dad.

Most of you know these things.

"Some of you know that I saw my dad kill a man. Some of you know that I found my mother's body when she died. Not many of you know that my dad was abusive—to both me and my mom. Not many of you know that my mom was having an affair."

Mae Whitlow stood and walked to the back of the room but didn't leave.

"Only a few of you—maybe really just one—know that my mom was sick, addicted really, and my dad was angry. You see, every story is intricate. Every story is lined with truths that are clear to the people who know them as truths. But the way you all know my story is not the way that I lived my story.

"The way that your story unfolded may intertwine with someone else's, but each of us is impacted in drastically different ways.

"Again, we are talking about testimony today. We are talking about how our testimony shapes our understanding of our own identity, but one thing I want you all to see is that testimony also can shape our understanding of the gospel and of grace."

I was really intrigued by where he was going with this, and even more surprised that he was speaking so freely about his past.

"Take out your Bibles if you have them, or you can use the Bible app on your phone. Or if you have neither, follow here on the screen. We have a screen today, folks. Isn't that awesome? We are going to read from the book of Acts today, chapter 9."

Gentry read Acts 9:1–20.

"Okay, let's talk about this and break it down. A man named Saul was a huge persecutor of Christians. He was killing them and mocking them. But on top of that, a lot of people don't realize that Saul actually had a very impressive background. He knew Jewish law really well. He had some clout, so to speak. On the road to Damascus, after Jesus had died, Saul was approached by Jesus, who shined some serious light on Saul and asked why on earth he was persecuting Him. Saul was made blind and stayed that way for days until Jesus got one of the disciples to take him under his wing."

He was so engaging. He walked across the stage, and his tone matched the intensity of the story he was telling. Gentry had been quiet in high school, but now he spoke with so much confidence.

"Jesus said to Ananias, 'Go, for Saul is my chosen instrument to take my message to the Gentiles and to kings, as well as to the people of Israel. And I will show him how much he must suffer for My name's sake.'

"Pretty heavy stuff there. I want to ask you guys a question. We are, after all, talking about identity here. We've got a few points to discuss about testimony. First, Christ will shine a light on your circumstances. Second, He will recover the blind—meaning, get ready to see all the things you have been avoiding seeing. Last, He will use your story, your life, exactly as it is and make you one of his chosen instruments."

Gentry preached that God made us as we are with a purpose in mind. Circumstances happen in life, both good and bad. But within all those circumstances, God will use them to further Kingdom progress. He explained that we use testimony to assign labels to ourselves, but God assigns grace and truth to who He wants to use us to become. I had gone to church with Lula for the greater part of my life and had never heard anyone preach like him.

"Saul's name was changed to Paul," he continued. "All this came about after Saul hit rock bottom. Jesus used this terrible situation, shone a light on it, and then told Saul that he was no longer going to identify as Saul. He was made new. So the question I want to ask you today is, In what way has your testimony changed who you are—for the better or worse?"

Several in the room were impacted already, likely recounting all the events of their lives that had led up to the molding of their character.

The primary thing that stood out to me about my own testimony was that I was unwanted. How was God going to use something like that?

CHAPTER 28:

Everybody's Good at Something

Mac Landry, 1984—I was used to attention from boys, but not boys like Josh Langston. He was the most popular boy in our school. I shouldn't have been too surprised, because I wasn't low on the food chain or anything, but he was going places. College—a concept that I had thought about but hadn't grasped as an actual possibility.

It sure sounded nice. Walking among ivy and brick buildings and studying into the late hours of the evening. But I couldn't keep my grades high no matter how I tried.

I flunked my fourth statistics test of the year—not because I didn't study. Mama and I had stayed at the kitchen table until about midnight practice testing. I was so proud of myself because despite my struggling, I managed to do very well on our practice quiz. I thought I was ready.

I sat at my wooden desk with my number-two pencil and listened to the sounds of the classroom. The ticktock of the clock distracted me further, and at a certain point, all I could hear was the loud breathing of the kid beside me. I looked around the room and saw everyone else focusing.

I tried my personal best, as Mama always told me to do. By the time the bell rang, I still had five questions untouched, and I was unsure about the answers I had put down for the other fifteen.

Mr. Rufty was the football coach and the youngest teacher in our school. It was his first year teaching, and he was fresh out of college. He was tall and good looking, and all the girls in school hoped to get his class.

Mr. Rufty smiled a kind smile as I put my test down. "I'm sure it's okay," he assured me as I walked out the door. I knew it wasn't okay.

The next day, Mr. Rufty asked me to stay behind. He told me to take a seat at the desk in front of his. I must have definitely failed the test. I was hoping he would give me a few extra-credit assignments to get back on track.

"I have to hurry. I think I'm going to miss my bus," I said.

"It's okay," he replied. "I'll make sure you get home."

He walked over and stood in front of the desk I was sitting in.

"You see, Mac, everyone is good at something. You may not be great at math, but you've got a lot of other great qualities."

It was really nice of him to say.

The final bell rang, and he walked over to close the classroom door.

He returned to my desk, and I felt his breath coming down on my face. I started to feel nervous. Slowly I was piecing together that I wasn't there just to talk about my grades.

He put his hand around my ponytail and pulled the rubber band out. Hair fell around my shoulder. I stared down at my hands, which were red from clenching my binder. I tried to get up, but he put his hand on my shoulder to push me back down to my seat.

He leaned forward while I was trapped in the desk and started kissing me. I pushed him with my hands, but he was holding my face still, and I was pinned into my desk. I picked up the binder and pressed it into his throat to push him away.

Mr. Rufty was angry. I stood up from my desk to push past him, and he slapped me in the face. Hard.

"There's not a single person in this school who would believe an F student over teacher of the year. Go ahead. Tell. I'll deny it until I die."

I turned to run out of the room, and he grabbed and ripped the bottom of my shirt before pushing me to the floor. I managed to get up and run out of the classroom, down the hall, and out the doors of the school.

I ran to Josh's house. Hair disheveled and crying, I slammed both of my closed fists on his front door.

He opened the door to find my shirt torn and makeup running, and he immediately pulled me in for a hug.

"What happened?" he asked.

"Mr. Rufty attacked me," I started. "He locked me in the classroom and started kissing me. When I pulled back to run, he grabbed my shirt and tore it. I ran here. What do I do?"

Josh looked at me for a second with fear in his eyes, like he didn't know what to say. And then he did the one thing I never expected him to do.

"You kissed our teacher?"

"No, I...I didn't kiss him. He kissed me. I didn't want him to. He attacked me, Josh." I tried to explain myself, but Josh looked more and more angry.

"Do you know who I am, who my family is?" he yelled at me. "This is embarrassing, Mac."

"I didn't plan it. I didn't do anything," I cried, my voice hitting a register I didn't think it was capable of.

"I've seen the way you girls look at him. It's gross. You probably asked for it. I'm so embarrassed." He was embarrassed. Of all things. I was attacked by my teacher, and he was the only person I had told. He was the only person I ever would tell.

"Just get out. Go take a shower. I can't look at you right now."

I walked home just as disheveled as I had run to him. When I arrived, Mama wasn't there. She must have been at the store picking up groceries for the week. I walked into my bathroom and showered with a pit in my stomach and arms that felt like all life had drained out of them.

When Mama finally arrived home, she brought in one round of groceries and asked me to grab some from the car to help. I stood still.

"Mac, I asked you to do something. You need to listen to your mama."

I paid attention this time and walked to the car to grab the milk and orange juice, shutting the trunk behind me.

As I sat the groceries down on the counter, she asked me about my statistics test. "Did you find out yet? How'd you do?"

"I'm just not smart, Mama. Sometimes people aren't good at math. I'm good at other things."

Not understanding what I was getting at, she hugged me. "Yes, I suppose you are, sweetie. You've got a lot of great qualities."

At that, I let Mama know I wasn't hungry for dinner and went upstairs to vomit. I never told her what happened that day.

As seventeen-year-olds, the things that worry us aren't always logical. I wasn't worried about whether Mr. Rufty would do it again. I was worried that I'd get in trouble. I was worried that Josh was breaking up with me. I was worried that my classmates would think that I instigated the kiss. I was worried that people would find out and get the wrong idea.

Josh approached me at my locker the next day. He was so attractive and wore expensive clothes and cologne already. He was the kind of boy who turned heads when he walked down the hallway. And I had his attention.

He leaned against the lockers and touched my shoulder. "You okay today?" Out of nowhere he had developed some sympathy. When I think about it now, I understand that this was narcissistic. At the time, I thought it was sweet.

"I'm hanging in there. I didn't go to his class yet today. I don't know how I'm going to face it."

"Let's just skip out. Let's get out of here during lunch. Just you and me. We will go to the lake with a picnic and get your mind off of things."

It sounded great. The boy of my dreams. A future college student. He was perfect in nearly every way. He squeezed my waist and told me to meet him behind the school as soon as the lunch bell rang.

He opened the door for me to get into the passenger-side seat of his blue 1976 Ford Mustang.

I felt so important in that seat. Then the blue-and-yellow jacket came off, and he laid it across my legs.

"I want you to have this."

I stopped focusing on what had happened the day prior and looked deeply into those baby blues while he smiled into my soul before we drove away.

He must have planned the day, because he pulled a blanket and picnic basket out of the car to put down by the lake.

"This day is about you." He laid the blanket down, and I sat on it while he handed me fruit and sparkling juice. "I would have gotten the good stuff, but my parents were home last night."

"No, this is perfect," I said as I looked softly in his direction. "This makes me feel so important."

At that, he leaned in to kiss me with his eyes wide open. He kissed me softly first and then aggressively as he arched my back to lay me down on the blanket. I don't remember us talking through the experience even once.

I just remember him being fast, and firm, and in charge of the situation. And I never said no.

After he was done, he stood up quietly and grabbed my hands to help me stand up. He folded up the blanket and grabbed the picnic supplies and put them back into the car. I thought we'd stay longer and eat, but he said it was time to go. He didn't open the car door for me, nor did he look at me on the way home. He dropped me off and grabbed my face and aggressively kissed me again.

I got out of the car and walked into the house to find Mama cooking. I walked upstairs for a shower and again said nothing about my day.

At school, you would have thought I was a ghost to him. But not to everyone else. Laugher erupted as I walked through the hallway and hushed whispers from girls who had pretended to be my friends filled the silence of the onlookers. Did they know about me and Josh? Had someone seen us?

I walked to Josh to figure out what was going on. He looked at me in the eye with anger on his face and said, "I can't believe you'd do this to me."

"Do what?" I asked. "What did I do, Josh?" I was genuinely concerned.

"You made out with our teacher." His volume and the continued laughs from the hall made me realize exactly what was going on.

I leaned in to whisper, "Josh, did you tell everyone?"

"Mr. Rufty was arrested this morning for having a relationship with a student. Everyone knows it was you."

The walls started closing in on me, and I felt dizzy. I ran out of the front door of the school while the principal and school counselor tried to get my attention and pull me back in.

Mama found out that day, too, when the principal and a police officer showed up on her doorstep. That night, she sat on the couch with my head in her lap, crying with me. She held my hair and told me repeatedly that it was going to be okay. I told her what had happened with Josh too. She fixed my favorite dinner, and we watched old movies until I fell asleep. We did that for a few days until I started to feel better.

About a month later, I missed my period. I sat on the toilet waiting for the lines of the test to tell me what I already knew. I wasn't lucky.

The day I told Josh, I was sure he'd come around and make it right. To this day, I don't know why I saw that potential in his character.

Instead, Josh looked me dead in the eye and said, "You sure it's not Mr. Rufty's baby?"

I didn't know how to react. The kids in the school knew Josh and I had broken up, and no one assumed that Josh had anything to do with this. I never outed him. Part of me held on to a hope that Josh would make the right decision and decide to be a father.

Mama tried to go to Josh's parents to insist they make it right. We sat on their back porch while Josh's dad grilled hamburgers. Josh stayed up in his room the entire time and didn't make an effort to come down to see what all the fuss was about. His parents didn't call him down or bring him into the discussion in any way.

As Lula and I got in our car to drive home that day, I saw Josh looking down at us from his upstairs window. I almost detected uncertainty and pain in his face.

Shortly after, while I was still pregnant, his whole family moved out of state. I never saw Josh again, and he never made any attempt to see me.

Mama agreed to let me get my GED so that I wouldn't have to go back to high school.

I knew it would be hard to meet this baby. I didn't know how hard.

The months leading up to meeting her were difficult. I wasn't doing a very good job being pregnant.

The night I went into labor, the pain was terrible. I knocked on Mama's bedroom door, and she ran out holding bags, telling me that we were okay and on our way. She was so excited to meet her granddaughter.

She helped me sit in the car and drove me to the hospital, where they set me up with an IV and a gown in a room of my own.

Mama handed me ice chips and rubbed my back while I sweated through each contraction.

Mama squeezed my hand and said that everything was going to be fine.

They held up the baby, and I cried, begging to hold her. They needed to cut the cord and clean her up, but soon she was lying on my chest while Mama helped keep her positioned that way.

Holding her was the most magical moment of my life. Despite how she came into this world, I knew the world would be a better place with her in it. I looked at her and saw enough of myself, but I also saw Josh. It didn't faze me at first.

"What's her name gonna be?" asked Lula.

"Rosling, like your maiden name, Mama." That was the only thing I knew for certain. I wanted her to have as much of Mama as possible.

Weeks after having her, I was still in pain, barely able to walk up the steps without hurting. I was still tender everywhere, bleeding, and it hurt my breasts and body to even take a hot shower.

Mama was as kind and as helpful as possible, but the pain was too much, and the fear of how I'd be as a parent grew overwhelming. I had dark thoughts about hurting myself, and it made me not want to touch Rosling. A few more weeks went by, and my mental state deteriorated further.

I couldn't even be in the same room as her. Mama had to take over to change her and feed her at night. I couldn't bear to pick her up.

As soon as I was well enough to drive, I packed a bag and kissed them both while they were still sleeping. I left in the night and cried my way out of town, hoping that I'd heal properly, both physically and mentally, before coming back to either of them.

Over time, the physical scars healed. Mentally, I'm still not sure I'm there.

I've driven through town almost yearly, close enough to the house that I could check in on both of them without being noticed. The love in my heart was never the problem. How can someone get past the fact that she isn't cut out to be someone's mommy?

I knew that Lula was the right person for the job. She had all the goods. Everything it took to be a solid rock for this baby.

I was a dumb kid without a husband who was weak enough to get taken advantage of two days in a row.

Yes. No doubt about it. Rosling was better with just Mama.

CHAPTER 29:

Judgment

Rosling, 2020—It was the first service where I'd be playing the keyboard in front of the congregation. My hands were sweating, and I asked the sound guy repeatedly if he would turn me down in the house so that the room could be spared from what they were about to experience.

He laughed and took me in stride but didn't do what I told him to.

I stood on the stage behind the piano, which was placed somewhat behind the other instruments and singers toward the middle of the setup. The drums were to start us out this time, and I was thankful that my first set would only include a few songs that I had practiced for weeks. We played a song about being children of God, exactly who He says we are.

"Middle C," I whispered as I positioned my hands to get started.

I didn't mess up, and I was looking for Lula's expression as we were finishing up.

The sermon started with Gentry playing a funny video of women gossiping on a porch. The room was erupting in laughter through the video. Gentry moved back to the middle of the stage.

"This is the third week in our grace and identity series. Today we are going to be talking about judgment. No one in this room is judgmental, though, right?"

More laughter emerged from every corner, and husbands elbowed wives while many looked around and narrowed their eyes at one another. At least the room was self-aware.

"Every person in this room has been judged before. And every person in this room has likely judged someone else. What's even crazier is everyone in this room has likely judged themselves. Maybe even today. Maybe you've decided that you aren't worthy of something. Maybe you've decided that you lack the skills or gifts to make an impact.

"When we spend time living in judgment, whether it's judgment of ourselves or other people, we aren't allowing God to do His own convicting. Further, we are making assumptions about how God feels about us.

"Are we so busy judging others as a defense mechanism that we don't notice the giant plank in our own eye? There are so many verses about not judging others, but what does it mean? Does it mean that we can just go along with sin? Does it mean that we should turn a blind eye to it? Or does it mean that the condition of our heart plays a part in all of this?

"What should our response to sin be? What should our response to our own condition be? If we walk around understanding the nature of sin—the background of sin, if you will—we can understand more about how to overcome it. If we walk around in judgment, we stop listening to what God wants us to do with the truths He's given us.

"Mark 5 tells us about a man who has dubbed himself Legion because he is possessed by many demons. He is shackled and cutting himself with stones. He is so strong that he wrenches his chains apart.

"Mark 5—Jesus and His disciples approach the shore where this man is. The disciples are trying to tell Jesus that they are on the wrong side of the tracks, but you know Jesus. He's kind of a rebel, right? They approach Legion, and let's read what happens next. Mark 5:7 is where we will get started.

"And crying out with a loud voice, he said, 'What have you to do with me, Jesus, Son of the Most High God?' For he was saying to him, 'Come out of the man, you unclean spirit!' And Jesus asked him, 'What is your name?' He replied, 'My name is Legion, for we are many.' And he begged him earnestly not to send them out of the country. Now a great herd of pigs was feeding there on the hillside, and they begged him, saying, 'Send us to the pigs; let us enter them.' So he gave them permission. And the unclean spirits came out and entered the pigs; and the herd, numbering about two thousand, rushed down the steep bank into the sea and drowned in the sea.

"The disciples are terrified and, of course, naturally judging the situation, said, 'No, let's not associate with that person.' Even Legion himself is like, 'Man, you don't want to come over here. I'm bad news.'

"But Jesus isn't afraid to get his hands dirty. He isn't afraid to take a situation that we have decided is dire and walk into it. That's what He does for us every day. We walk around as Christians trying to make the decisions ourselves. Know an addict? Well, nope, he's not fit for the Kingdom. A convict? Nope, him either. God is going to do His own judging, and yes, He has given us His Word and the conviction of the Holy Spirit to help us to understand what sin is and how to stay away from it. But who are we to decide who is good enough for Jesus? The way scripture puts it, He cares about all of His children and will even leave the ninety-nine sheep to find the one lost sheep every time, right?

"The hardest part is that some of us do this to ourselves. We look at our past and say that we are unfit for the King. And yes, that's pretty true. None of us have done anything that is deserving of His love and presence, but even the righteous are bringing filthy rags to Him. Not one of us is worthy. But that's why He came! That's why, folks.

"Bow your heads with me. I'm going to pray us out as the musicians come back to the stage."

He had his head bowed but then looked up for a second to scale the room.

Gentry prayed, and I played piano through his talking until he walked off the stage, and we ended the service with a final song.

With Mama, I knew I was sitting in judgment of someone I'd never known. I was also judging my own worth, or lack thereof, based on that same person's actions. I decided it was time to call Mama. That afternoon I dug through Lula's desk drawers and found an old phone number. I hoped it would work.

I dialed the number and waited.
"Hello," she said.
"It's Rosling."

CHAPTER 30:

Gentry Fishing

entry, 1995—Dad woke me up before sunrise and told me to be real quiet so that we wouldn't wake up Mama. I could tell he hadn't showered the night before, and his breath smelled like the glasses he and Mama usually left out on the living room tables. Brown liquor.

"Where we going, Daddy?"

"Fishing." We were both smiling, with our eyes partially lighting up the dark with excitement.

I got out of the bed as quickly as possible and walked to my dresser.

"No, no time for that. Just go in your pj's," he said.

I laughed, giddy at the fact that I could leave the house in my pajamas. Mama would have made me change first.

"Just throw on them boots right there. Let's go," he whispered, and I tried to quietly hustle through the excitement.

He turned the front doorknob so slowly that it didn't make a sound. We lightly crossed the front porch and walked down to Daddy's truck. I still don't know what time it was, but the sun wouldn't make its way up for hours.

The boat was hooked onto the truck already, and we backed out real slow and quiet, not even turning on the stereo until we were far enough for Mama not to hear us. I kept thinking it was nice that Daddy was trying to let Mama sleep. She was always up before everyone else, so I knew that she'd appreciate it.

"It's low tide," Daddy said as he pulled up to the lake. He told me to hurry, and I climbed into the boat so I could ride in it while he lowered it into the water.

It was already a great day.

He moved the truck into a parking spot, climbed into the boat, untied us, and we rode off into the water—still no sign of the sun.

He drove fast and threw a life jacket at me, laughing.

As I put it on, I giggled. We anchored the boat near a small island. Daddy got out a few poles and set them up with bait. He told me to run around the island while he set us up. After he got the poles ready, he leveled them on the side of the boat. He said we'd see them pull if anything bit.

Daddy grabbed a camera from the boat and asked me to find a good tree to take pictures near.

"Look, that's a great climbing tree."

One thick branch swung down low to the ground, low enough that I could swing myself onto it after a few tries. I edged myself as high as I could before I got scared. Then I sat still, looking at the boat on the water and peering into the distance, knowing that there was nothing else out there for miles. It was our day.

Daddy pulled out two Cokes as the sun started to rise.

"Here son. Breakfast. Don't tell your mama." He smiled.

We clinked the glass bottles, and I watched him go off into his mind, staring out at the water. He was sitting up straight with the sun on his face. It was the happiest I'd ever seen him look.

"What's the best thing to fish for, Daddy?"

"It depends on what you're hungry for, I suppose."

I waited for him to go on.

"But really, it's not always about catching the fish. Sometimes it's the experience of it. It's slowing down and forcing yourself to have patience and appreciate your surroundings. It's a chance to go off into your head. We all need that."

Those trips became more and more spread out until they stopped.

The day I met Rosling, I was supposed to go fishing with Daddy. He was called into the shop early that morning by one of his employees who couldn't make it in. I still put on my normal fishing clothes and boots, figuring maybe he'd take me when he got off work. I met Rosling instead, and I'd never get a chance to go fishing with Daddy again.

When I met Pastor Thomas, he introduced me to a verse from Matthew 4:19 that says, "Come follow me, and I will send you out to fish for people." Both types of fishing require passion and patience.

CHAPTER 31:

Rosling Fishing

osling, 2002—"Now, if you're worried over the elements, you're not gonna catch a single fish," said Lula. "You have to get over being uncomfortable sometimes. It's character building."

"What's wrong with my character?" I asked, only partially interested in her answer.

"Nothing's wrong with it. You just need to exercise it to stay humble. Kind of like running track. You have to stretch your hamstrings first. In order to have humility and empathy, and in general to be a nice person, you have to sometimes do things that stretch yourself."

"I have empathy. But I'm also freezing."

"You can't go hoppin' around in this water." She pointed at all the fish that didn't seem to be hungry. "You're letting the enemy see your struggle. Never let the enemy see your struggle."

Lula had grown used to giving me unsolicited snippets of wisdom, but I didn't trust her this time. She wanted me to stand knee-deep in freezing cold creek water to catch trout of all things.

"Are we even going to eat what we catch?"

"We will always eat what we catch. Unless it's not a fish, of course."

I tried to fashion my fishing pole to lean on one of the larger rocks, but it wiggled into the water each time.

"Just look at how beautiful it is out here. You know for sure that God put all this together. Can you imagine dreaming this up?"

She stared across the creek at the rock wall towering up toward the clearest sky you'd ever seen. Creek water ran around larger rocks while smaller stones and fossils collected beneath our bitter feet.

The scenery wasn't what I was worried about. I didn't understand why we had to stand in the water. We could fish just as easily outside the creek and might last even longer, in fact. Akin to this, I was a teenage girl and opted not to be excited about anything. In the event that we'd run into a boy at the creek, I was wearing my best pair of cut-off jean shorts and had braided my hair before putting on my snap-back.

I had declined breakfast that morning and felt my stomach protesting. Thankfully, we had snacks, but I didn't know if I'd earned one yet.

Trout fishing was just one of the things Lula thought a girl needed to know how to do. If you can catch your own dinner, you don't need to depend on anyone. Just like changing a tire or doing your own taxes.

The year before, she had taught me how to cook, drive, balance a checkbook, and properly tell a person no. The long and short of it is, there's no laughing, no smiling, no hesitating, no negotiating, no explaining, and no guilt. Many of our life lessons entailed me learning a necessary life skill. Her favorite, a repeat in the playlist, was how to properly maintain a well-poised poker face.

In my teen angst, I fell subject to the standard hormonal fluctuations, which led me to eloquently explode all my feelings onto Lula. She could take it. I'd yell and cry, and she'd carry on with her task as though I were just a ghost in the room. It drove me crazy that she never fought back. She'd wait until I finished freaking out and then would not even touch the subject.

My fishing line began to tug, and I began reeling in the line quickly. She jumped over and grabbed my hand.

"Don't let the fish see your excitement," she said.

"I know you're kidding, Lula. The fish? Are you really worried about the fish figuring out that I'm excited?"

I laughed at Lula and looked down into the clear water at my toes seeping through mud and rocks.

"No, what I'm worried about is you getting your hopes up thinking you're about to catch a trout when what you're really about to get is a soggy boot. You have to set proper expectations in all aspects of life. You see this water? It's flowing fast, and you can see it moving madly around the rocks, yes?"

I nodded.

"Well, look at our legs. We are standing still while the water panics and runs about. But we are standing firm."

Lula put her hand on mine and helped me to slowly reel in.

"I understand I need to stand firm. But why can't I get excited?"

"Just don't get excited about a boot that's masquerading as a fish. When you know it's a fish, you can be grateful. Until you know it's a fish, always be mentally prepared that it may in fact be a boot."

Rosling, 2020—Gentry and I sat on the steps of the porch in silence, waiting for my mom's car to pull into the driveway. I didn't know what to expect. Every time I faced the unknown, I always followed Lula's advice and expected a boot instead of a trout. The more I thought about it and quietly pondered the situation, the more I wished I hadn't actually called her. What good would it do? If she actually cared about Lula, she would have been around a long time ago.

At this point in time, I was the only one who could be taking care of Lula, who should be taking care of Lula. I started to resent and regret taking that leap of faith.

"I sense you having second thoughts," said Gentry.

"What in the world? Are you clairvoyant?"

"Ah, you're wearing your smart-aleck hat today, are ya?" He grinned at the empty driveway.

"Well, you seem to think you can read my mind. Like always."

"No, I just noticed you squeezing the step of the porch like it's done you wrong or something."

I didn't feel up to having a conversation about my feelings or having said feelings analyzed. We hadn't discussed our kiss yet. It might have been easier to talk about that. I kept quiet, as I was debating whether to speak to him about my mom or kiss him again just for the sake of shutting us both up.

A silver Honda pulled into the driveway slowly. I couldn't make out her face, but the window was down, and I could see curly blond hair just like mine was blowing in the breeze. I stood up and thought about my next move. Should I leave the porch or wait for her to come up? How would I say hello? Then I remembered. Trout versus boot.

She parked far away from the porch even though you could drive right up to it. I wondered how many times as a young teenager she had driven up to the porch from a day at school. How was it that we were both raised by the same woman? What possessed her to leave her mother and daughter and never return?

My mama stepped out of the car and stared at me while she stood next to it, holding onto the hood for a moment.

"Rosling." Her inflection was more observation than question. How could she possibly know I was Rosling?

"Yes." I couldn't get more out of my mouth but felt like an idiot for standing there quietly.

"You look wonderful," she said. "Really beautiful."

I still didn't speak.

She and I looked at each other for too long before Gentry finally broke the ridiculous silence. "Would you like to come inside?" Thankfully he hadn't forgotten his manners.

"Yes. That sounds good. It's been a long drive," she said. She walked up to the porch step and smiled at me as she passed and walked into the house behind Gentry.

When I placed the call to Mama, I learned that she had married a nice guy named Chet when she was eighteen, and they moved to Florida. Chet passed away earlier that year from heart disease. For the past ten years they had owned a salon with an apartment upstairs. The day I called her, she had just closed on the sale of their home and business. She was happy to hear from me and said she'd be able to make it back within the week.

We sat down in the front sitting area while Gentry went into the kitchen to pour us some water.

"So when's the last time you saw Lula?" I asked.

"It's been a while. I think you were a young girl at the time." I was ten. I remember that party like it was yesterday. She looked out the window when she said it. I wanted her to look in my direction. To acknowledge what she did at that birthday party.

I became silent again and got annoyed with Gentry for taking so long.

"Have you always called her Lula?" Mama asked me.

"Yes."

"How come?" she asked.

"Because she was more than a grandmother to me. I would have called her Mama, but she always called you Mama. For as long as I can remember."

Mama became quiet after that. I did too. I wasn't trying to avoid conversation, but it was difficult to speak without getting angry. Gentry was taking his sweet time pouring water, probably on purpose. We waited several minutes for him to return.

He finally walked back into the room with the waters, and I glared at him for leaving me alone with her for that long.

"So, how sick is she?" Mama asked.

Per my request Gentry did most of the explaining. "Lula has Alzheimer's," he started. "She is still doing pretty well. She knows who we are, and she follows her routine to a T. But she also has troubles with remembering words and how to do small tasks. The short-term memory is really what usually suffers. It's the most noticeable thing to go. It's what makes them typically repeat themselves."

I grinned at him, knowing he was regurgitating my previous explanation almost perfectly.

"Did they say how long she has?"

"Well, the thing is people don't typically die from Alzheimer's specifically. As far as the progression of the disease, though, it can be years of doing fine, and then sometimes the deterioration is quick."

"Where is she right now?"

"At the bingo hall," I cut in, knowing that I'd be creating some confusion.

Both of them looked at me, and Gentry raised his eyebrows and smiled.

"She plays bingo?" Mama asked, shocked.

"She's at that bingo hall nearly every day. You would think it's her second home. I'd say she's there almost more than she is here."

"When did she start playing bingo?" she asked.

"She's not playing bingo," Gentry said. "We're renovating the building. It's going to be our new church building."

"What happened to the old building? God, she used to bring me there every Sunday as a kid."

I kept thinking of our dual childhoods. She looked like she could be my older sister. The same woman with the same routine had raised her in the same house. I never imagined the day that I'd sit across from her, but now that I was finally in it, I felt like I was looking at an older version of me. A less reliable, selfish older version of me, that is.

The more I sat there, the more I wanted to know about her. Why did she leave? Who was she before she left and after she left? Did she ever want to come back? Lula had always given me the good stuff about her. She never shared the full story of why Mama left and who my real father was.

"I'm going to go ahead and leave y'all to it," Gentry said.

He stood up and squeezed my knee. Then he kissed my cheek before walking out.

"Is that your boyfriend?" asked Mama, raising her eyebrows.

"No. He's the reverend."

Mama sat still and quiet for a while before either of us spoke. Lula had one of those ticking clocks that sang every time it hit the hour mark, and I was wondering if I'd go crazy before the next time it went round.

"Rosling, I know that I have a lot of explaining to do."

"You don't have to explain anything. You weren't here. Now you are. Lula's sick, and I don't have the energy or time for drama. I just want her to know that the people she loves are around her. I didn't just do this for me."

"I'm really glad you called. I know it must have been hard."

"No, the call itself wasn't that hard. Watching Lula get excited over you being around is going to be hard. Watching her wonder why you disappear will be even harder. So if you don't plan on sticking around, don't even bother to let her see you."

With confidence in her voice, she answered me firmly. "I'm sticking around. I know I wasn't your mother, but I was her daughter. You don't know much about me, and I know that most of that is my fault, but you don't have to worry. I'm sticking around."

"Good. She'll be back within the hour with Del. Until then, if you'd like anything, you can help yourself. I'm sure you know where everything is."

"Which room is yours? I'm wondering where I can put my stuff."

I showed Mama to her room and made tea. Lula and Del walked in the door within the hour, and Lula had no problem recognizing Mama. She dropped her purse on the floor and walked right to her with tears in her eyes. They hugged for what felt like forever, and Lula sobbed. Mama and Lula stayed up later than I had any interest to. I let them catch up while I read in my room alone.

The next morning, Mama and I woke up first and let Lula sleep for a while.

Mama was putting dishes in the sink when I walked in the kitchen.

"I know this is not my kitchen, but old habits die hard, so just bear with me while I move around."

"No, it's okay. This means I won't have to do them later. Carry on."

She made me a cup of tea. It was the first cup of tea. I thought I should take that in, whether I was ready to or not. Something about her handing me tea in Lula's house brought me back to the reality that we were both products of the same loving woman. I needed to try harder.

"I'll give you ten questions today," I said.

"Ten questions?" she asked.

"Yes, I know that we need to start this process slow. Just ask me ten things today, and I promise to answer honestly and without sarcasm. I'll try my best."

"Thank you," she said. "Let me take the next thirty minutes to think about the best ones to start with. What about you? I know you have questions."

"I don't want to know anything yet. I'm not ready."

"Okay, that's fine. I'll go first."

CHAPTER 32:

Breakthrough

entry, 2002—The high school at night was always more fun than the high school during the day. I had found a solid group of friends, and by solid, I mean they were consistently bad too. They didn't have the grade point average that I did, and I was mocked for being a good student. Something about them making fun of me for being a good student made me want to cut up even more than I was naturally inclined to.

It was 1:00 a.m., and I had sneaked out of Mike and Janice's apartment.

"Do you have the glue?" Toby, a little on the clumsy side, was grabbing at his twisted ankle. We hadn't been running yet. He had twisted it on his walk up to the back of the building.

"Yes, three tubes of it," said A. J. He was two grades above Toby and me. He had a girlfriend, was always in trouble, and could drive. We still don't know whether he was supposed to drive or whose car we were in, but at the very least we knew that he could drive, which was more than Toby and I could say.

"Okay," I said. "What's the plan here?"

"You and I will glue the locks to as many doors as possible, and Toby, you be the lookout."

"Why do I always have to be the lookout?" he asked.

"Because you break your arm just by getting out of bed. There's no way you can be trusted with an actual challenge."

He sulked and shook his head but nodded and walked to the top of the hallway while A. J. and I got to work.

"Remember," said A. J., "if you just put a little glue over the front of the lock itself, no one will be able to get into the classrooms, and school will be canceled."

Toby's laugh echoed through the hallway, and I grabbed a few tubes of the super glue and started on the opposite end from A. J.

We covered a lot of ground in a three-minute period while Toby started pacing around the top of the hall.

"You done yet, Gentry?" A. J. asked as he held out another tube of super glue and walked toward Toby. "We still need to hit the offices and the second floor."

As we turned the corner to head to the stairwell, the school's security alarm went off. We began running down the long front hall toward the exit. We made it out the front of the building and started down the concrete stairs that led the way up to the entrance.

Toby, too clumsy for the challenge, tripped over himself and slid down a few steps face-first, busting his chin and bending his arm the wrong direction. It didn't take a medical professional to confirm that the arm was broken. Toby screamed in pain.

Sirens in the distance fought Toby for volume as he cried and begged us to help. He was inconsolable and far too big for us to carry.

A. J. shrugged, screamed at Toby, and then kept running. I sat down on the step next to him, patting him on the back and telling him it would all be okay. It would be okay for Toby. He'd likely need a cast, and the arm was definitely broken, but at the end of the day, he'd get a slap on his wrist, and his parents would ground him. Knowing that I'd disappoint Mike and Janice, this was the first time in years that I'd felt real guilt.

The cops pulled up in front of the school and saw us sitting on the steps. Toby left in an ambulance, and I left in the back of a cruiser.

Mike picked me up from the station a few hours later. I expected to be punished or put back into a group home, but it didn't happen. When we got home, he heated up the pasta Janice had made earlier that night. They really did eat a lot of pasta. When he set the plate in front of me, I didn't know what to say. He sat quietly while I ate.

"I'm going to go get a shower. I've got to get to work in a few hours. Need anything?" he asked.

"No. Thank you though," I responded.

"Okay. I guess you succeeded, because school's canceled tomorrow."

"I'm really sorry."

"Listen, Toby's going to be fine. They know A. J. was there because they had cameras. As far as you're concerned, though, you've got the most to lose."

"I'm the one who doesn't have anything to lose."

"The way I look at it, you may not have your original family. But you've got a huge future and the chance to make a family of your own one day. You are clawing your way out of a hard hand, and one day this all will be memories and lessons. I know you're a straight-A student. You're smart, Gentry."

"It doesn't matter if I'm smart."

"It does matter. It matters a lot."

"Look, I'm not your son. I know that you are good people. I'll try to chill out from now on. But you don't have to pretend to care this much. I will do better though."

"Listen. Janice is not ready to have this conversation with you yet. It's been very hard on her. About a year ago, we lost our son in a car accident. He would have been graduating high school this year. You aren't technically our son. In fact, we lost our son. But the way we see it, we lost our son, you lost your parents. We all have a chance to be a family again. Chances like that don't come around every day."

At that, he got up and went into his bathroom to shower for work. I went online and looked at four-year college applications.

I stayed with Mike and Janice until I graduated high school. They sent me money through college for various needs like laundry detergent, deodorant, gas, and more. Mike was able to attend my college graduation as well. They became like real parents to me. Eventually they moved across the country to Colorado when Mike's work transferred him. I was lucky to have them through my final year of high school and through college.

Gentry, 2020—I was already awake, which is very out of character for me. Typically I don't wake up to a fire alarm, but something had me moving around my house at 2:00 a.m. When the phone rang and I heard Del's voice on the other end, I had to make sure I wasn't in some odd dream. He was in jail. For breaking into the high school. Baby Eleanor, who was sleeping in the backseat of the lookout car with Del's friend, was also at the police station.

"I'll be there in thirty minutes," I said, hanging up and doing my best in the middle of the night to dress myself.

As a kid, I had walked through the doors of this police station many times, but it was never through this entrance, and typically I was being escorted. In fact, this was the first time that I was on the pickup end of the scenario. When I walked in, I was greeted by Miss Rhonda, someone I made good friends with as a young kid. She always sneaked chips into the cell for me while I waited to get picked up. She smiled with all her teeth and came out from behind the door to hug me.

"I thought they was lying. You are really back home? Tell me this. Are you really a pastor now?" She squeezed my shoulders and started sizing up my new look.

"Yep, I'm a pastor."

"Boy, you cleaned up good, didn't you?" She laughed. "So what you doing back here, then? I know you didn't just come up here to see me."

"Well, you would have been worth the trip, Rhonda, but no, I came to get someone out."

"Oh, those tables. They are turned now, ain't they?"

She told me to take a seat while she arranged Del's release. When she opened the door again, Del was on the other end being escorted by an officer. He released him into my care, and I signed for him. They hadn't informed me yet what would happen that evening with baby Eleanor.

We sat in the car quietly before I started the engine.

"Why didn't they call your parents?"

"They tried."

"What were you doing in the high school?"

"I was supposed to be stealing the scales." Drugs. That was my biggest fear.

"There are some problems you can't get people out of. Drugs is one of them."

"I'm not on drugs. I was going to sell the scales. I needed the money since I got fired from the diner. I haven't been able to work as often during the day, and I've been taking care of Eleanor more for my mom, so I was just trying to make a little extra cash. I'm sorry."

"Del, what's going on? Is your mom around?"

"My mom has only been home a few days a week for the past five months. Dad left a long time ago, and we haven't heard from him. I've been raising Eleanor. By myself."

I listened quietly while he spoke and realized I should have listened to Rosling as she was trying to warn me.

"I don't want to fail Eleanor, but I'm starting to realize that I can't take care of her the right way."

This was why he wouldn't tell me why he had dropped out of school. The signs were there, but Del was a black box and filled in no gaps for me. Until now.

"I'm eighteen. I don't want my baby sister to be in the system. I want to raise her. But I know that I'm not capable of doing it the right way." Del was crying into his shirt.

I understood everything he was saying. He was coming to me for help, and I knew that I had a decision to make, and the path forward had to create a solution that would allow Del to be an eighteen-year-old and prevent his sister from growing up without him.

I had one idea only.

Mae Whitlow.

Mae had more room in her life than anyone else I knew. I knew she'd be cantankerous about it, but I also knew she'd never have a cold enough heart to leave a young boy from the church without a place to stay. She didn't have that in her. She was a tough nut to crack, but I was confident that maybe Del was the man for the job.

After I made the call, Mae fussed at me for dialing her so late. She paused when I made the request but then quickly said that it was the Christian thing to do, so I should arrive as quickly as possible. I pulled up to her house, and we both got out to walk up.

"Do you have any other clothes?" she asked Del. "Because all these band T-shirts are not gonna do it. We've got to clean you up and set you straight. I'll take you to the outlets tomorrow to buy some decent pants, for crying out loud, and I'm cutting your hair. There will be no fight about that, do you understand me? Breaking into the high school, of all things. Do you at least go during the day when you're supposed to be there?"

Del smiled at me. He knew how to handle Mae and didn't mind anything she threw at him. If she fed him daily, they'd be a match made in heaven. My next step would be getting Eleanor to Mae. That would be more difficult.

I told Del and Mae I'd be meeting a plumber in the morning and asked Mae if she was going to come out to help too. She laughed and told me that plumbing was not in her repertoire and that I'd have a better chance of getting a kangaroo in a pair of tennis shoes.

I left Del and Mae to it and decided it was too late for me to try sleeping. I went to the church building and began to pray—for Del, for Eleanor, for Mae, for all of them.

CHAPTER 33:

The Right Thing

Gentry, 2020—Eleanor and Del were probably just waking up. Knowing Mae, they'd be on a schedule. I was sure she'd feed them well, get everyone dressed before sunrise, and Del was probably already signed up for his GED. Baby Eleanor was in fantastic hands.

I waited outside Del's house for almost three hours, starting with a coffee and then finally eating through the sandwich, chips, fruit, and protein bars I had packed for my lunch that day. I was supposed to be renovating, but this was bigger.

The one-story brick house looked well cared for. The lawn was freshly cut, and I could tell that someone had been caring for it. Del was doing a good job.

When Maggie Chase finally pulled into her driveway, I could tell she was under the influence or had been the night before. She opened the door of her '93 Toyota Corolla and emerged with broken flip-flops, jeans, and a blue-and-yellow Liberty High hoodie that said "Class of '03."

I approached slowly, knowing I might freak her out if I didn't keep cool.

"Hi. Maggy Chase?"

I held my hand out to shake hers, but she declined. She looked at me like I was a cop. I suppose in this situation, I probably gave that vibe.

"Yeah. What can I do for you?" Maggie rifled through her purse while she continued the walk to her front door.

"Del and Eleanor aren't home. Del was arrested last night. They are both safe now, but I didn't want you to worry when you went in."

A smile tightened on one side of her face while she continued to dig in the purse to find house keys. I didn't want to share that they were on top of her car because it might have shortened our discussion.

"What'd he do?"

She didn't even ask about the baby.

"He was caught at the high school stealing property from the labs."

At this, she laughed and shook her head. "Okay, and Eleanor—what'd she steal?"

All this was a big joke. I found myself getting angry.

"Look, Maggie, I've been up all night and all morning talking to the right people and filling out paperwork. It's clear that you have a lot going on, and you look pretty busy. But I'll cut to the chase. I don't want Eleanor to end up in foster care and for Del to waste his life away because he has no resources."

"So what do you want?" She looked up at me and left the contents of her bag alone to focus in on me. "I remember you," she said. "I knew you looked familiar. We went to high school together."

"Yes, we did. I'm back in town. Actually, I'm the pastor who's rebuilding the bingo hall. Turning it into a church."

"Okay, Pastor." She found humor in this, which did make sense. "What exactly can I help you with?"

"Del is eighteen. Eleanor needs attention, and Del needs to finish high school. He mentioned that you can't be here as often as you'd like right now. I have a friend who can help."

"How exactly can your friend help?"

"Instead of Eleanor ending up in foster care due to obvious neglect, Del and Eleanor can remain together, supervised by a foster mom, who will eventually be able to adopt them. The friend I mentioned is speeding up that process for me. At least as best as she can. But the only real guarantee right now is that Eleanor and Del stay together and Eleanor is not bounced around from home to home."

"Why can't she stay here?"

"When Del was arrested last night, the right people—or wrong, I suppose, if you look at it that way—got wind of Del and Eleanor's current setup. You being gone, no food in the house, narcotics, et cetera. It doesn't look good."

She wiped a few tears before they had a chance to make their way to her chin.

"Your kids have a chance of a better life. If you clean up and decide that you want to be a mom again, I can help to make sure that you can at least be in their life."

"What gives you the right to come on my lawn asking to keep my baby? I should scream."

"Scream if you'd like. I'm only trying to help."

"Why would I sign my baby over to some lady I've never met?"

"Del would be with Lula every day, and Eleanor would be safe and have a roof and clothes and food."

She paused for a second. "I used to be something special," she said.

"I remember. I think that somewhere inside, you probably still are."

"What happens if I want to see my kids?"

"We will work it all out. Can you just come with me to go get all this sorted out? The way we're doing this now will keep Eleanor out of the foster system, and it will allow you to come back when you're ready and be their mom."

"So you are going to help me?"

"Yes. By the way, your keys are on top of your car."

After she grabbed her keys, we got into my car and drove into town to see Anna Briggs, my former case worker.

CHAPTER 34:

Court

Rosling, 1995—I was a character witness in the trial for David Lee. Lula and I had to drive for over an hour to get to the courthouse. Lula's pink heels click-clacked against the black-and-white tile and echoed louder than swift justice.

Gentry sat in a nice suit with another grown-up woman behind his daddy, who was next to several lawyers. I only had to answer a few questions, they said, and I ought to answer them honestly; otherwise, it was a crime. I understood that just fine.

Lula kissed me on my head and said that she was sorry I had to do this, but it was the right thing to do.

"I call to the stand Rosling Landry."

I approached and sat down on the wooden seat next to the judge, who seemed about ten feet tall sitting next to me. The jury sat to my left, and the lawyer approached me like he said he would, giving me my instructions again, but this time before the judge, jury, Gentry, and his daddy.

"Okay, Miss Landry, can you tell me if you've ever seen the defendant, David Lee?" He pointed to Gentry's daddy. Gentry stirred in his seat, giving me the firmest stare down I'd ever received.

"Yes, I have."

"Okay, and have you ever seen this man, Bill Whitlow?" He held up a picture of the man whom Gentry's daddy shot that day. It was a nice picture. I noticed Mae Whitlow and Lula were sitting together. Lula was consoling Mae as she cried into a handkerchief.

"Yes, I have seen both of them. Together."

"Can you tell me what you saw the day that you saw them both together? Do you remember the date?"

"I don't remember the date, but I was running outside near the old covered bridge in Liberty, and I met Gentry. We saw the defendant drive by fast in his blue truck, and he got out and fought with the man in the picture."

"Can you tell me what happened during the fight? Did anyone get hurt?"

"Yes." I moved uncomfortably in my seat, and Gentry began to bite his thumbnail and look at his daddy. "I saw the man who got out of the truck, the defendant, shoot the man in the picture—Bill."

"She's lying!" Gentry got out of his seat and began punching the table in front of him. "Daddy, I'm going to help you. She's not telling the truth. I wasn't there. I didn't see nothing that day. She's lying!"

I looked at the judge, who began to use his gavel while the courtroom officers removed Gentry. His daddy stood to watch his son being pulled out of the courtroom, and tears welled in his eyes.

Mae stayed to watch the rest of the trial, but Lula wanted to get me out of there.

"Rosling, it's okay. You didn't do anything wrong," Lula reassured me as we walked to the car. The only thing I could hear in my head all week was Gentry screaming that I was a liar. He never testified during the trial. There was too much evidence against his daddy, and at this point it wasn't good for Gentry's mental health to sit on the stand. He wouldn't have told the truth anyway.

CHAPTER 35:

Questions

osling, 2020—"Do you like dill pickle chips?"

"I don't know. Is this one of your questions? You only get so many before I cut you off."

"No, this doesn't count. I just want to know because I'm making Lula lunch."

Mama hung the top half of her body around the corner to the front room, where I was practicing songs for the week. I had to get used to someone else making the lunches.

"Oh, I guess I'll take a handful. Do we have Coke?"

"No, but I'll pick up some cans later if we need them."

We had found a rhythm, mostly dictated by the needs of each day. Mama had been with us for a few days and had been asking very targeted questions to get to know me better. Most of them were good, and I tried to give unbiased, clear accounts, but some of them were ridiculous. She asked me what type of car my high school boyfriend drove. When I looked at her puzzled, she raised her hands and said, "I'm just trying to get a visual of you growing up."

I resented having to answer basic questions, but she had been doing virtually everything around the house, and

Lula loved her being there. I couldn't complain, though it was hard having a third person around the house. I kept expecting her to go home.

"You're playing really well," she told me as she set down a plate of food on the coffee table next to the piano.

I thanked her before eating the sandwich. It was a croissant with turkey, Muenster, avocado, tomato, and mayo.

"I do have one new question," she said.

"Okay, I'm ready."

I turned and faced her. She had on dark jeans and an old T-shirt from church camp. I was surprised that she hadn't outgrown it.

"Did Lula ever talk about me?"

Her eyes were so bright, and her curls were bouncing around like springs.

"Yes. She talked about you a lot until I was a teenager and I made her stop. It was very difficult to hear about the person I'd never get to know."

"Oh. Okay, I understand."

"I know a lot about you already, in fact. Just from her constant chatter. She missed you."

"I understand that must have been hard."

"Is that one of your questions?"

"No, it's an assumption. You don't have to respond."

"I did."

She nodded and got up to let me finish my sandwich. "Hey, you want to watch a movie together later after Lula goes to bed? Just the two of us?"

I thought about it long enough to make it awkward. "Yeah, but you can't ask me questions during the movie because it makes me crazy."

"Noted." She smiled and bounced out of the room.

We settled onto the couch after Lula went to bed for the evening. I made popcorn, and Mama had picked up the Cokes I'd asked for earlier that day.

"Okay," she said. "Now to pick a movie."

"I have my first question," I said.

She immediately turned to face me and sat with her legs crossed on the couch in anticipation.

"Please."

"What's your favorite movie?"

She laughed and looked up to the ceiling. "When I want something light, it's *Sweet Home Alabama*. When I want to think or cry, it's *Shawshank Redemption*."

"Okay, I think we'll get along just fine," I said.

It was easier to get to know her as a friend first. This would have to be enough for now. It was better than remembering that she was the mother who had never been around.

"So, before you put on a movie, help me with these details," said Mama. "Gentry's mom was having an affair with Mae's husband, so Gentry's dad shot him?"

She moved a pink pillow onto her lap and shoved a handful of popcorn into her mouth.

"Yes." She was just trying to catch up, but I felt like we were gossiping.

"And you witnessed it?"

"Yes."

"How did you get past it?"

"I didn't, and you're out of questions for the day."

CHAPTER 36:
Lula's Eightieth

Rosling, 2020—"I told you both that you aren't allowed to look better than me."

Lula feigned frustration through her wry smile, watching Mama and me move about the house putting ourselves together for the party. Lula put on the kettle while I debated which of Mama's dresses I'd like to wear.

"Please take this one," said Mama. "It will look beautiful with your eyes and hair."

She handed me a dark-green lace A-line dress with cap sleeves and an open back. It was very pretty and looked a lot like the dress I had stolen from Lula's closet as a child. It wasn't too snug and was about an inch above the knee. I thought back on my high school dances. Lula was always the one to get me ready for dances.

"I don't have any..."

"Shoes?" she asked, handing me a pair of black basic heels.

"Perfect."

I gave her a light smile and went to my room to pull myself together. As long as I considered her a new friend, living together was becoming easier.

I was having a good hair day, so I left my curls as is and dabbed a small amount of perfume on my wrists and neck before spraying and jumping through a haze of it. I stuck to ChapStick only because I couldn't stand having anything caked to my face.

I walked out to find Lula and Mama dressed and ready to go. They looked great, which didn't surprise me. I didn't expect to see Gentry come out from behind the fridge door. He was in a bow tie, and his hair was clean cut, but at my recommendation, he was growing a small beard.

"You look beautiful," said Mama.

Gentry nodded.

We arrived at the party, and the parking lot was packed. A band was set up and playing before we even walked in. Trays of finger foods were placed end to end throughout the church, and people were already having a great time. A three-tier hummingbird cake with cream cheese frosting was being visited by hungry little hands that couldn't wait for it to be cut.

Round tables were adorned with centerpieces of flowers and candles. Not lit, per Mae's suggestion.

Lula didn't waste any time. She grabbed onto me and Mama and pulled us in the direction of the dance floor. We laughed and obliged.

The entire family has rhythm; there's no question to it. We moved around that floor to hits from Lula's younger days, and she sang every word. She ate up every moment.

I danced solo with Mama a few times. She'd grab my arms and twirl me around while she shook her hips and mouthed the words to songs that everyone knew.

Everyone was having fun. Even Mae Whitlow joined us on the dance floor with baby Eleanor in her arms. She had managed to get Del into a tie.

Mama said she needed to take a water break and had a seat at one of the empty tables. I filled a plate of food and joined her.

"Rosling, I want you to know something," said Mama.

"You don't have to explain anything to me. In fact, I don't know how well I'd handle it." I wiped my chin with my napkin and clenched it for good awkward measure.

"I don't want to explain. There's nothing I can do that would explain leaving. I have a hard time explaining it to myself most days. I just want you to know that I missed you. I didn't live these thirty-five years enjoying my life without you. I was a broken person...I am a broken person, and I thought about you every day."

I didn't know how to answer her, so I placed my hand on top of hers while she cried. I didn't cry. I couldn't cry. I heard the words and felt like she meant them, but deep down I wanted to scream at her for making Lula raise me alone, and I wanted to scream at her for making me feel unwanted. For taking away a confidence that I'll never get back.

"I know I'm supposed to say something," I said. She looked up from crying and wiped her eyes to focus on me. "I will never really be able to accept anything you say about leaving. I will never be able to look at you and tell you that it's okay. It's not okay. But I can say, and really mean it, I'm so glad that you're here now."

Her face changed from sorrow to warmth at that, and she squeezed my hand that was clenched around the tissue.

"I have one more thing to tell you," she said.

"What's that?" I laughed.

"You seem to be making an impression." Mama subtly pointed in Gentry's direction. He was looking down at his plate but every few seconds would look up in my direction.

"Mama, I've been making an impression on him since I was ten years old." I stood up to walk toward him. "Sir, you seem to be fascinated by something at my table. Can I help you with anything?"

He tilted his head to the side and put down his plate on the table before grabbing my hand and pulling me to the dance floor.

His right arm wrapped around my waist, and his left arm slid from my shoulder to my hand, which he held out before he started swaying slowly.

"So you can play guitar. You're a pastor. And you can dance?"

He spun me out from his grip and pulled me back in closer. "I'm a man of many talents. But you—you have talents I didn't know about."

"And what might those be?"

"You have this ability to make my knees feel like they're gonna buckle from underneath me." He stopped dancing but kept holding on while he looked at me and continued speaking. "I can't imagine what it's going to be like if you ever decide to leave this town again. But I already have a pit in my stomach thinking about that."

I held in my breath and started to feel flushed. He made me feel the same. I knew very well that I wasn't going anywhere, but I was having a hard time telling him that.

The party went on, and people dropped in and out.

"Rosling, I'm headed out!" Lula shouted over the remaining voices in the room.

"Lula, what do you mean you're out? It's your party!"

"I know, I know, but mostly everyone is leaving, and we've eaten cake. And I'm sure as heck not gonna clean this mess up. Mae's agreed to take me home. She's gotta get that baby in the bed."

Mae stood behind her with Del, who was now holding a sleeping Eleanor. She waited peacefully while Lula said her goodbyes.

"Okay, but are you sure? I can come. I can leave now."

"No. Don't think about it. Someone has to help Rev get this place up to snuff for service Sunday."

"What about Mama?" I asked.

"She's coming back too. We're both tired."

At that, Lula and Mama walked out with Mae and her new entourage, and I looked back at Gentry, who hadn't broken his concentration on me.

"I'll help you clean up."

The crowd emptied out quickly after Lula left, leaving me, Gentry, and a few others putting chairs back into their normal places, emptying food platters into containers, taking the trash out, and sweeping.

We stood around talking. Gentry answered a lot of questions about the message he would be preaching Sunday, and I sat on one of the chairs listening to how passionate he was about teaching and discipleship.

We had lingered too long, and it was time to leave. Everyone else had gone on long before, and the last few people trickled out to their cars, heading in their respective directions.

"I'll obviously bring you home," Gentry said, laughing. He was my ride to Lula's party, and the rest of the group had cleared out.

We rode back in silence. When he pulled up to the house, he got out of the car to let me out and walked up the porch steps with me to the front door.

"Rosling, I'm sorry if I crossed a line earlier."

"No. No lines were crossed. I'm just trying to figure out what to make of all this. We have such a weird history, and I don't want to jump into anything that will create more heartache."

"Is this about me cutting off your hair when we were kids? Or is it about the murder thing? Because I think you're being a little sensitive about both of those things."

I laughed and went to hit his arm in a flirtatious way, and he pulled me in and kissed me.

History or no history, things were starting to feel right with him around.

"Gentry..." I pulled back for a second. "Where do we go from here?"

"Marriage?" he half joked.

"Seriously. Can we really do this? You and me? Would this ever work? My faith is extremely weak, and you...well, you have serious faith. The kind of faith that really must be directly from God, because there's no other way to explain it."

"But here you are. Taking about God. Talking about faith. And my faith is directly from God. I had enough faith to seek Him, and He took it from there. I can't promise you that it will be that easy for you. I can't promise you that a walk with Jesus is always a clear and thornless path, but my faith saved my life."

"And you want to save mine." I shook my head, understanding that I was a project.

"Are you kidding, Rosling? I don't just go around kissing people. I'm not trying to date you because I want to save you. Ideally both would happen, but that's not my angle here."

"I don't want to be anyone's project. I don't want to be saved. I'm going to be fine, and I don't need you or Jesus or anyone else to make that happen. I've got everything under control."

"Rosling."

"Listen to me. This won't work, okay? I am sorry. Believe me, I really am."

I walked inside, shutting the door gently behind me.

CHAPTER 37:
What We're Looking For

Rosling, 2020—The dust from Lula's party had settled, but I had too much adrenaline to change and go to sleep yet.

I checked in on Mama's room, and she was sound asleep. I took my heels off and threw my hair back into a high bun before I went into the kitchen to investigate the fridge contents. Barefoot in my pretty dress that I didn't want to take off yet, I ate a few grapes while I walked upstairs to Lula's room to check on her.

Opening her door, I found a perfectly made bed. Lula hadn't made it into the bed.

I checked in my bedroom and the front and back porches. She wasn't in her closet or the restrooms or the dining area either. I checked the front again and saw only Mama's and Lula's cars. Had she taken my car?

I called Mae, and she answered right away.

"Do you know what time it is, Rosling?"

"Yes. Did you drop off Lula this evening, Mae?"

"You saw me leave. Of course I dropped her off."

"She's not here. She must have gone off somewhere."

Mae began yelling for Del to get up and drive her into town to look for Lula.

I ran outside, hoping to see any indication of her departure.

I started running with my phone past the water on the right side, over the highway bridge into town. I called Gentry, but it went straight to voice mail.

I screamed Lula's name into the empty night. It seemed like I was the only one alive in the world. No lights came on, no neighbors came out, cars didn't pass. I called 911 on my phone and looked each way down the street, trying to figure out which way she might have gone. What if she got into an accident? What if she drove into to the water?

I ran fast in the direction of the old covered bridge. The bridge where I first met Gentry that day. The air was cold in my lungs, and my feet were sinking into the earth. Mud flew up and hit my legs, and I cried as I searched. I looked up at the sky and talked to God.

"I have been in your company for a long time. We have some friends in common, but I've never gotten to know you. I don't know whether we have enough in common to be friends, but because we both care about her, can you please help me find her? Please help me, God. Please. I can't lose her this way."

Headlights from the covered bridge pulled up and parked, shining brightly in my direction. A tall man in a bow tie emerged from the vehicle. Gentry. I ran over to him and jumped into his arms, crying.

"She's not home, Gentry. She's supposed to be home, and she's not home. What if she went into the woods or the water?"

He put his hands over my hair and face and started whispering to calm me down. "Listen. You hear that?"

Sirens erupted in the background.

"They're searching right now. We'll find her. I swear we will find her. Please. Breathe."

The very notion of someone telling me to breathe at that moment made me lose all composure.

He grabbed my hand and walked me to the passenger side of his car. "Let's go. Let's keep looking, okay?"

He drove. He drove for hours around town until we saw daylight.

I felt like at this point we'd never find her. It was too late.

Gentry walked into a diner to get us a few coffees so that we could keep going. I sat in the car waiting for him, completely drained of all effort and energy.

He returned to the car and handed over the coffee.

"Let's head to the house for a few minutes. You can take a quick shower and change, maybe eat something, and then we can get back to it."

"I just don't understand. If we haven't found her yet, we aren't going to find her anyplace good. There aren't enough businesses that she could have wound up at. It's late, and everything is closed. She's been wandering all night and has probably ran out of gas by now. She doesn't have her wallet. And it's cold."

Gentry nodded and seemed to understand the weight of what I was saying.

When we pulled into the drive, there was still an empty spot in the driveway next to Lula's and Mama's cars. Mama was sitting on the porch.

"Lula's missing," I said in an accusatory tone.

"What do you mean? Where would she have gone?"

"That's what people with Alzheimer's do. They wander."

"Oh my gosh, what can I do?" Mama stood up quickly as the police drove into the driveway.

"Well, for starters, you could have been listening for her. Paying attention." Gentry reached for my arm as if to tell me to stop accusing Mama, but it kept coming. "You should have been here. For everything. All she ever did was take care of you, and you just let her run off."

Mama didn't argue. She cried, but she did it silently. I regretted everything I said as I said it. It wasn't her fault.

The police confirmed they found my car empty on the side of the highway. They were still looking for Lula and asked us to confirm what she was wearing and to show them pictures from the party.

We went inside to change, with the intent of going back out to look for her.

I walked onto the front porch first and saw Lula walking up the driveway in her dress from the night before, shivering. She had to have been in the forty-degree weather for the entire night.

We brought her inside and grabbed her socks and blankets while Mama called an ambulance to bring her in. We didn't know what had happened to her, but likely the cold did some damage, so we wanted to get her properly checked out.

When the ambulance arrived, they asked who wanted to ride with her. Mama stepped up, and I jumped into the back before she had a chance to speak.

They hooked Lula up with an IV and brought her internal temperature down. The left side of her face was dropping. I knew she was having a stroke.

"Lula, listen to me," I said. "I need you to stay here. I need you, Lula."

Lula looked at the paramedics and then back at me. There was nothing I could do.

"Lula, tell me again. Tell me the thing about mustard seeds. Tell me, Lula. Tell me." I needed her to keep fighting. The paramedics edged me back to my bench seat and continued to work on her.

We reached the hospital, and she was wheeled very quickly through the emergency room and into a room where doctors and nurses quickly rallied around her to try to make some difference. I wondered if it was worth it and what good it would do at this point. I stood gawking, unable to fix it.

A few days passed, and she wouldn't hold down food. Her advanced directive and will were very specific about not resuscitating and not forcing treatment. If she was on her last leg, she was on her last leg.

Lula wasn't able to speak but made discernable noises and acknowledged when I was in the room next to her.

Gentry and Mama alternated visiting us. I stayed in the chair next to Lula almost the entire time we were in the hospital aside from when I had to take a bio break. Mama frequently read to Lula, and Gentry picked her fresh flowers every day.

One of the nights, I was watching Lula sleep. *Law and Order* played quietly in the background. It was an episode we had watched while I was growing up. It didn't matter what I put on the television. She wasn't going to react.

Gentry sat on the chair next to mine and grabbed my hand. The human touch took the wind out of me, and I turned to cry into his chest. He held the nape of my neck.

The next morning, Lula's doctors let me know that it was time to send Lula home. She'd be considered hospice from here on out. It was only a matter of time.

Gentry picked me up, and the hospital arranged for Lula's transport back to the house.

"If it's okay with you, I'd like to stay and help out for a few days," said Gentry.

I agreed and set up blankets for him on the couch. I was emotionally drained and needed sleep, so I lay down on Lula's bed next to her, waiting for her to wake up, waiting for her to look at me and tell me it would be okay. She didn't speak. She lay still next to me.

Days went by. I had done this for a living, but it was much harder knowing that the patient was my Lula.

Mama and I worked together to change her, feed her applesauce, wash her sheets, and sing to her.

Mama had the voice of an angel. She sat on the bed next to Lula, holding her hand and moving hair out of her face, singing "It Is Well with my Soul." Gentry stood at the doorframe and raised his eyebrows at me while I grinned at Mama, perplexed.

"I'm sorry I left you, Lula. Thank you for everything." Mama cried and continued singing.

The next day, we'd wake up early to dress ourselves and Lula for Gentry's sermon, knowing it would likely be Lula's last time at church.

CHAPTER 38:

Starting Over

osling, 1995—"Baby girl, sit right here on this bench and put your hands on these keys."

I sat on the wooden bench, and Lula placed her left hand on my right hand and moved my fingers where they were supposed to go.

"Always remember middle C."

"Lula, you keep telling me middle C. I already know that part. I'm never going to learn this."

"Not with that attitude. Listen. If you can remember middle C, honey, you can always get back to where you started."

"Why would anyone want to get back to where they started? Wouldn't you want to be farther than that?"

"Well, yes. But the thing is, we humans make a lot of mistakes. We mess up and lose our way. When we lose our way, it can be hard to find ourselves down various paths that look appealing, that look like they'll be shortcuts to the place we're hoping to land."

"But middle C does what?"

"Middle C doesn't ever lie. Middle C is when a person says, I'm going to start over and understand that it doesn't matter what song I was just playing or how out of tune it was, I can start again."

CHAPTER 39:

Forgiveness

osling, 2020—Gentry stood at the podium quietly while we shifted from the stage and found our seats. He rested one hand on the edge, and I noticed that he didn't have any notes with him. The new building was officially renovated. There was a handful of remaining tasks that needed to be finished, but it was in beautiful shape.

"Today is the final day of our identity and grace series."

He started walking around the stage, looking at the different faces in the audience.

Mama and I wheeled Lula in her chair up to the front row to watch the sermon. We had barely spoken since I blamed Mama for Lula getting lost. I was impressed that she had stayed after I tore into her. Now I was just trying to find a window to talk about it.

"We are talking today about something that many of us find impossible. And it makes sense that we find it impossible because it feels very much out of our control. Forgiveness."

He continued as he returned to the podium, still without notes.

"I can tell you about the verses that say that if you don't forgive, your sins will not be forgiven. I could do that. I could tell you about how we don't deserve forgiveness, but Christ still offers it. Yes, I could tell you all about that."

He paused and looked directly at me.

"There is one thing today that is critical for you to take home with you. Above any verse I can tell you, above any story I can tell you. Above anything else. The root of forgiveness—the backbone of what has to happen in order to forgive—is love."

The room was quiet.

"Many people think that if you forgive, you are saying that what the person did is okay. Many may say that when you forgive, you have to forget what happened—act like it never happened. These two things alone can seriously deter people from the ability to truly forgive."

I felt like I was doing this with Mama. Treating her like a new friend instead of addressing the pain head-on. It was making me resent everything more.

"Here's something crazy. You can forgive someone who's not even sorry. All of this, all of how you approach forgiveness, is dependent upon one thing. It depends on where your forgiveness is rooted. Here are a few quick calls to action.

"One—be confident that God is going to sort it all out. Ever heard that expression 'it will all come out in the wash'? We can't assume we understand all the psychological and situational conditions that led to us being the way we are, but we can accept that there are some things that aren't going to make sense to us."

He was right. Mama leaving would never make sense to me. Murder would never make sense to me. I had been stuck for a long time trying to comprehend chaos.

"Two—be comforted that God is still working on you too. A lot of us aren't in great shape when God reaches us. And even after we have a relationship with Him, we are serious works in progress.

"Three—be consistent in making forgiveness and love actions, and not emotions."

I looked at Mama, watching Gentry intently. I wondered at that point if she had anyone in her life that she needed to forgive. It was at that moment that I couldn't wait to ask her about her life. There was so much I wanted to know.

"We know from our verse that love keeps no record of wrongs. We know what it means to have the emotions of love. What does love mean to you? Love is a decision. If it is emotion based, it's something else. It's something we are gaining from and give up on when it doesn't work out to our advantage. In the same way, forgiveness must be action oriented. It's something you are doing.

"So what do you have to do with your forgiveness? Do you have to run to the person and tell them that everything they've done is all okay? Do you owe that person anything?

"No. We need to consider that the act of forgiveness is not just about setting the other person free. Forgiveness, true forgiveness, is allowing God to work in your heart and help you grow. He's molding you. Some of His best work is done by softening your heart and breaking down your walls. He's not doing that just so the other person can have a 'get out of jail free' card. He's doing that because it's difficult, if not impossible, to accept the forgiveness of Christ when we can't extend it to others."

There was no question that my walls were breaking down. I knew that everything Gentry was saying was right.

Gentry invited the band to come up to play one more song and encouraged the congregation to spend a few moments in reflection and prayer.

"When we look at our name—Christian—let's understand that that literally means 'little Christ.' In order for us to grow and be more like Christ, our character has to become more like His. Gentle, humble, graceful, forgiving. We have to embody love. Fight for the hopeless. Forgive the sinner."

Gentry invited Mama and me to bring Lula to the front for the congregation to pray.

"Here's Lula, everyone. I'm betting most of you have been impacted by the grace of Lula at some point in your life. She's been a huge part of this community, of this church, and of my own growth in relationship with Christ. Lula was put on hospice a few days ago. As hard as this is to say, there may not be many more Sundays that we will get to have Lula here in the church, so I'd like us to all join together in gratitude and prayer for what Lula has done for us as a community and as a church."

We played a final song, and some came up to the stage and began to pray on their knees. Several people from the congregation came up to pray with them.

Mama and I held hands, and each of us placed one on Lula's shoulders.

"I'm sorry I said it was your fault," I said. "I don't know how close I am to forgiving you for everything else, but I know that I'm going to try."

"I know," she said. "No rush. I'm not going anywhere this time."

We walked out of the church, pushing Lula in her chair, and parked in the front was the same blue Mustang that I'd been seeing all over town.

Mama looked uncomfortable and asked us to take Gentry's car back to Lula's. She said she'd drive home separately and pick up groceries on the way.

"Yes, no problem. Are you okay?" I asked her.

"Yes and no. Rosling, this is not going to be easy to say, but that man is your father."

She pointed at the man leaning up against the Mustang, and I immediately saw the resemblance.

My mouth must have gaped open wide.

"I'm going to get to the bottom of this, and I know I have a lot of explaining to do, but for now it's probably best if I talk to him first."

I didn't protest. I had bigger things to tend to at the moment. Mama walked in his direction, and he stood tall as she approached the car.

I heard him say "Can we go somewhere and talk?" as Del and I were getting Lula situated in Gentry's car.

CHAPTER 40:

It Is Well

osling, 2020—When we got home from church, Gentry and I got Lula set up in her bedroom to sleep. I was eager to catch up with Mama about her interaction with my father, but that wasn't my priority at the moment.

Lula fell asleep fast, and I walked to the kitchen to search the cabinets for some kind of sustenance. With the way Lula used to cook after church, my body and brain had conditioned themselves to be starving after hearing the Word of God.

Defeated, I leaned with my back against the kitchen sink. Gentry entered the kitchen and stood facing me after checking the fridge and finding nothing. We stood quietly for a moment with the afternoon sun peering through the kitchen window, bringing a yellow glow to the clean room. We hadn't used this kitchen in weeks, it felt like.

"That was a really good sermon," I finally said, breaking the silence.

He didn't break his own silence yet and just nodded slowly, as if it would take too much energy to speak.

"I mean, I really feel like it helped me. I'm starting to get to a really peaceful place mentally. Almost joyful. I should be falling apart, but I'm not. I feel like I would be if it weren't for you. Well, I mean if it weren't for God."

"Are you going to stay?" It was abrupt, and I realized that he was worried about me leaving, the same way I had been worried about Mama leaving.

"Why would you assume I'd be leaving?" I asked.

"When you don't need to stay for Lula," he said.

"I'm going to stay. This has always been my home. And it's time to know Mama," I said.

"Any other reason you want to stay?" he asked.

"I want to stay with you," I said.

He moved forward and leaned against me, the sink supporting both of us at this point. Before I could speak, he was kissing me. The screen door opened, and Mama walked in the house with groceries. He backed away but kept eye contact. She walked into the kitchen to put down the bags and realized she had just walked into something personal.

"I can go if you need me to," she said.

"No," said Gentry. He broke eye contact and put away the bread, milk, and eggs while Mama started tea and turned the stove on to fry some chicken.

We ate, and then Gentry went home to Mae's for the evening. His days on the mattress in the kitchen of the church had ended, and Mae had opened up one of her many spare bedrooms to him. Mae, Del, Eleanor, and Gentry—one big happy family.

Mama sat me down on the sofa, and we drank tea and talked until two in the morning. She told me that my dad's name was Josh Langston and that he had embarrassed and abandoned her during the loneliest time of her life. She told me about the afternoon she got pregnant with me. She told me about feeling isolated and having postpartum depression. She told me that she was always afraid to come home.

I remembered myself in high school, awkward and constantly worried about the opinions of others.

It was like a spool of ribbon unraveling. I wished so badly that she had allowed Lula to help her during that time. There was no going backward, though. She had been through something traumatic, and it was my choice of whether to press on toward a future with her in it. I needed to do it. For Lula, for Mama, and for myself.

Josh, my father, asked for forgiveness that afternoon. He came back to town with the intent of finding her. Instead, he found the daughter that neither of them had stuck around to raise. He told her that he wanted to meet with me, and she told him that she'd ask me how I felt about it. With everything else going on, I wasn't ready to meet him yet. Maybe soon.

That night, I lay wide awake next to Lula. It was harder to fall asleep than it had been the nights prior. I placed my hand on Lula's and turned to face her while she lay in bed with her eyes open, taking in the room.

She began to hum with her mouth closed the melody of "It Is Well With My Soul." Tears flowed from my eyes and hers, and I knew that for just this moment she was here with me still.

We both fell asleep, facing each other. The next morning, I woke to find that Lula had passed in the night.

—~—

We buried Lula right before sunset in the shady part of the yard. It seemed like every person in the town made their way through her yard that day.

Mae baked a fruitcake and brought four jugs of sweet tea. She had a confidence about her with a baby on her hip. Her hands were full, but she seemed at peace.

"This ought to do it," she said. "If we don't have enough fried chicken later, I will drive and get some more."

"I think we'll have plenty," said Gentry. "Mae, you have a great heart."

Mama and I looked at Mae and then again at Gentry. They were having some kind of a moment, so Mama and I walked out of the room to let them speak.

"I'm sorry about your mama," said Mae. "And your daddy. And your whole childhood, Gentry." Mae broke down into tears and clung tight to him.

They hugged for a few moments, and I could hear him telling her that it wasn't her fault.

To lighten the moment, Mae squeezed his arm and said, "I'm gonna need you to do something about these kids you threw on my lap, Gentry. Del's testing my patience with his ever-growing pile of dirty band shirts."

"As in the bands are dirty or the shirts themselves are dirty?"

"Both, Gentry. Both."

I found my way into Lula's prayer closet. Everything was pristine. The Bible and a notepad sat on the windowsill, and fresh air crept in from outside. I sat in the chair and realized it was almost spring.

Tucked into her blue Bible was a letter that Lula had written for me to find.

> My dear Rosling,
>
> I've currently got my wits about me, so I thought I'd write you while I still can. I may be losing my sense, but I'll never lose my sense of humor, sense of direction, sense of self—even if I lose these things by the world's standard. I'll never be too far off the path because I'm not the one orchestrating the steps. You see, all these bad things that happen—God is not causing them. We can't look at our Lord and think that He wants us to lament. He doesn't. In fact, we know from scripture that He weeps with us. Jesus gives everything that happens, both good and bad, a purpose. He doesn't just make our paths straight, but He also seamlessly constructs a system of roads that connect us to others who need to know him. You asked me one day if I had any questions or anything I needed to know

before I passed on. I don't have any questions, Rosling. I've seen it all unfold, from the steps of my porch to the ringing of gossip in my ears to the lives that have fallen apart in front of my eyes and then been put back together in a way that is not possible by anything other than grace. Ah, grace. We just can't get enough of it. Now, stop crying. Go have some tea. Make some for Gentry too. And forgive the boy already.
XOXO, Lula

I could envision the dirty feet of a wide-eyed ten-year-old running quickly from this house in the direction of a boy who would grow up in the same town but under much different circumstances. I could see Lula's full body leaning out of the window while she yelled to me and drew me back in to her home. Our home. I could see that every road I'd ever run down, both literal and figurative, had led me to this very chair in this very room, and there was something amazing about that. For the first time—maybe ever—with faith the size of a mustard seed, I closed my eyes, and I prayed.

C H A P T E R   4 1 :

Something New

Rosling, 2022—"Mama, we have to start soon."

She'd been helping me get ready since 9:00 a.m., and I could see out the window that people were already taking their seats in the backyard. Some were shaking hands and standing around catching up while the music played, and Gentry's old friend Pastor Thomas made his way to the altar to wait.

Mike, Gentry's final foster dad, stood on the other side while Janice sat across from Gentry. She was already crying.

"Do you think he'll come?" Mama asked me.

"Gentry's daddy?" I asked. "I'm not sure, but I really hope so. Gentry's been pacing around all week anticipating. They've talked three times on the phone since Monday. Long conversations too. Like a bunch of girlfriends catching up and gossiping."

"What do they talk about?" She was entertained.

"Fishing, mostly. They're planning an offshore trip this summer. Just the two of them."

Of all the people anticipating the arrival of Gentry's daddy, Mae Whitlow was the one I was most worried about. Gentry had sat her down several times to give her pastoral therapy of sorts. She walked out on three of their sessions, but by the end of it, he had seen a ton of growth. Mae had officially adopted baby Eleanor, who was now three years old, and for good measure Del asked if she would adopt him by way of ceremony. He was an adult, so technically it didn't matter, but Mae still cried and rejoiced that she had not one but two babies. She even offered to pay for Del's college. He decided to become a worship pastor.

Del's mama found her way into prison when she ended up in the wrong passenger seat during her boyfriend's armed robbery. Del and Eleanor visited her multiple times, and she was on her way to getting clean.

Mae Whitlow took a few trips to the prison herself. In fact, Mae and Gentry took a ride together to David's parole hearing and fought hand in hand to get him released on good behavior two years early. She worked hard on the forgiveness process but was still pretty cantankerous about it. Naturally.

I knew it would be hard for her, forgiveness or not, to sit near the man who shot her husband. But we are all capable of grace that can surprise us if we really are thoroughly rooted in the source of it.

I saw David get out of a cab in his dark-blue tux and walk up to the altar to stand next to Gentry and Pastor Thomas. They hugged for a long time, and he and Gentry both wiped away tears. Holding Eleanor, Mae walked directly up to David and smiled at him while she grasped his hand and wiped away a few tears of her own.

The most beautiful thing that day wasn't the backdrop of Lula's begonias against the creek's edge. It was the sight of broken people mending in the wake of unspeakable losses and mistakes.

It was time.

"Let me fix your lips, honey." Mama was really great with makeup. She had even purchased her own building to open a new salon. She already had a list of clients. Her plan was to move out of Lula's after the business was up and running. Gentry would be moving in after the wedding, and Mama knew it was time for her to make her own way. But this time she'd be doing it in Liberty. As for me, I'd recently been hired on to run the local nursing home.

She adjusted my lips and fixed the rest of my face before checking the bustle on my white lace gown.

Handing me a bouquet of lilies, she kissed me softly on my cheek and told me I was beautiful. We squeezed each other's hands and walked toward the staircase.

"Wait a minute, Mama," I said, and ran back to Lula's prayer closet. I grabbed Lula's Bible and sat the lilies down on the table.

"I'm going to walk down the aisle with this instead," I told her. The Bible was old, blue, and borrowed. My faith was new.

When we reached the bottom of the stairs, Mama nodded in the direction of my father and then hugged me before walking down the aisle to take her seat in the front row.

As for me, I would be taking this walk alone.

I looked out at the crowd of faces who knew and loved Lula and thought for a second that she might be the glue, the glue that had brought all these people together and into the presence of Jesus. Then I looked at Gentry and decided that maybe it was him. Whoever it was, we were all responsible for the good and the bad. We were all responsible for the love that had been spread, for the forgiveness that had been extended, and for the lives that had been rejuvenated by taking a step back and acknowledging that it's hard to be human. It's hard to find grace.

One step forward out the door, several more down the steps toward the altar, and plenty more along the beautiful and unknown path.

ACKNOWLEDGMENTS

I'm thankful for the little girl who taught me about mustard seeds, and I'm thankful for a family that reminds me every day that sometimes we must borrow faith from one another.

Made in the USA
Columbia, SC
08 August 2023

214.14168R00145